FIVE TO TWELVE

Edmund Cooper

FIVE TO TWELVE

G. P. Putnam's Sons   New York

PART ONE

RENDEZVOUS

I have a rendezvous with Death
At some disputed barricade.

—ALAN SEEGER

ONE

It was a fine autumn evening. Stars hung in the sky like a frozen stream of diamond dust, the larger and nearer ones presenting a glittering illusion of mobility, as if they twisted slowly on invisible wires.

The air, fortunately, was still—fortunately, because Dion Quern hung by his fingertips from the edge of a roof parapet half a mile over London. One decent breath of wind and he would go hurtling to his death at thirty-two feet per second per second. It would not be an altogether bad solution, he reflected. There were worse ways of solving unfunny equations than dancing briefly through a warm sea of darkness to the ultimate dark.

But somehow he knew there would be no wind. Those who look for death have to wait patiently till death finds those who look.

He had been sunbathing on the roof of London Seven all afternoon. It was a pleasant way of spending the time—apart from the fact that he had become very hungry. But even if he had had any lions, it would not have been safe to chance the express pan again. Unattached sports attracted too much attention.

The hell with it! A little hunger was a lovesome thing. It sharpened a man's perception. Presently, with luck and a fair degree of poetic license, he would have lions aplenty. Then he could shuttle to a restaurant in one of the other London towers, gorge himself to satiety, accept the advances of the first unrepugnant dom, and in the morning take himself along to the nearest clinic for a badly needed time shot.

Such was the philosophy of Dion Quern, age forty-six, as he maneuvered himself inch by perilous inch to the balustrade on the balcony of the two-hundred-and-fourteenth-floor apartment he had chosen in London Seven. Anyone who could afford to live on the top floor of one of the London towers must be absolutely dripping with lions. Whether they were plastic lions, gold lions, or precious stones didn't matter a coprolite. All that mattered was that he should quickly lay his hands on the trove and depart without hindrance at Mach three.

There was no light from the apartment. So far as he could judge, during the last couple of hours there had been no sound, no any goddam thing. *Ergo* the box was uninhabited. The ferret was doubtless flushing rabbits in the plains.

Only a high-powered dom could drip the lions necessary for such a box. Dion hoped she was fat, flabby, and a hundred plus. He hoped she was coming to the end of her time shots and that she would die in a fit of senile ecstasy when next her favorite sport went riding.

He pulled himself over the balustrade and collapsed in a thankful heap, breathing heavily. Nobody had yet paralyzed him, he had not been electrocuted, and if there was an infrared system, it had—as yet—done nothing to promote the cause of justice at all.

But what the hell! Why waste lions on elaborate keepout systems for top-floor boxes. Nobody but an idiot would try to force them externally.

Enter Dion Quern.

The French window looked easy. It was easy. Too easy. He forced it and slipped into the apartment.

And then his number came up.

4

The lights went on and a dom wearing very little but a small laser pistol that pointed disturbingly at his navel said, "Hi, sport. I've been waiting quite a while. There were times, even, when I thought you might disappoint me. Now relax very gently and you may possibly avoid burning."

Dion let out a sigh and stood quite still. Laser pistols were fearsome things. Apart from blinding you, they could produce quite nasty little flesh wounds. He imagined blindness and instantly became a devout coward. Then he dismissed the possibility with a shrug. In this day and age what dom in her right mind would disfigure, maim, or incapacitate a less-than-repugnant sport.

"Who are you?" she went on.

"Will Shakespeare."

Damned expert, this one. She deflected her aim, pressed the button for a split second. He looked down in amazement at the smoking needlehole where the trews covered his thigh. Then he felt the pain. There would be one hell of a blister, presently.

"Dion Quern," he said hastily.

"Age?"

"Forty-six."

The woman laughed. "Stripling boy! You should know better than to play games with the grown-ups."

"Go ride yourself."

The woman laughed. She was very attractive when she laughed. If you cared for that sort of thing. Hell! Be gracious, even in defeat. She was very attractive anyway. Nearly six foot tall, about a hundred and sixty pounds of perfectly formed Amazon, and she couldn't be a day over seventy-five.

"You picked the wrong box, stripling. There are even pressure meters built into the ceiling. I've been waiting for you for some time. I'm the CPO for London Seven."

It was Dion's turn to laugh. He had scored three lemons. Of all the hundred thousand boxes in London Seven, he had to choose the one occupied by the Peace Officer. He would have been better employed as Robin Hoodlum raiding Scotland Yard for the Crown Jewels.

"What are you?" she demanded. "You're obviously no genius of the snatch trade. So what sort of genetic joke are you?"

"Dion Quern," he repeated solemnly, "jongleur extraordinary—and failed delinquent."

"Jongleur?"

"Troubadour."

"Troubadour?"

"Meistersinger."

She put a blister on his other thigh. It was a bigger one.

"God ride you, I'm a poet," he confessed irritably. "A reactionary scribbler. Now kindly hand me over to the dry cleaners, and I'll bid you a very good night."

"Not so fast, my stripling meistersinger. The night needs no time shots. We will talk a while. You may even aspire to the giddy heights of interesting me."

Dion was willing himself to stay upright. But the hunger, the futile exertion of climbing down from the roof—to say nothing of the laser burns—were cumulatively somewhat degrading. He began to sway slightly.

"You look pale, little one. Are you afraid of indecent advances?"

"I'm hungry," he sobbed. "I'm just plain bloody hungry. Also tired. I couldn't make it even if you tried."

"Tut-tut. What problems," said the Amazon. But her voice had softened. She picked up a combination purse lying by the side of her four-poster bed and slipped the laser pistol into it. Then she went across to the vacuum hatch and spoke into the pick-up.

"Half of brandy—*Remy Martin,* perhaps—a bottle of good hock, say the *Rampant '67,* cold chicken, green salad, French bread, and accoutrements for two. Five from the time of order. . . . Oh, and black coffee. Out."

Then she turned to Dion and indicated a restful-looking chair. "Drape yourself, love. It's been a hard day's nocturne. Forget the high drama. I'm Juno Locke."

6

"Stunned, of course," said Dion formally. He sank gratefully into the chair.

Yes, Juno Locke, Peace Officer of this parish, was quite attractive—if you cared for that sort of thing. Sometimes he did. Sometimes he didn't. Sometimes he wanted to scream.

Theoretically, he should have surprised her. In practice, he hadn't. She hadn't even bothered to cover her breasts—which, under the circumstances, was less than an unveiled insult. He tried to hate her, but it cost too much energy. Besides, he was damned hungry and she wasn't a day over seventy-five. It was the older doms that were the worst. They ran you dry, then howled for more. This one looked as if she never had to howl. Blonde, beautiful, and probably as tough as any two sports he could think of. Thank Marie Stopes she hadn't yet tried any rough stuff.

"You're not bad," said Juno, eying him critically. "You're not too bad. I might even decide not to hand you over to the psychos. . . . If you amuse me."

"Retarded maternal impulses?" he suggested with malice.

She should have been outraged, but she only laughed. "The name is Juno, not Jocasta. How would you like to be raped?"

"Not until after the brandy—unless you have a better anesthetic."

"That's my little troubadour," said Juno. "I'm beginning to like you."

TWO

Toward the end of the twentieth century, birth control ran riot. Contrary to the laws of probability, the proposition of repetitive history, and the prognoses of philosopher-psychiatrists—and despite the most comprehensive and insane buildup of lethal instruments in the history of man —there were no major wars. So birth control was the obvious biological solution.

That it came to be so easily accepted as a solution, even in such places as China and India, is a mystery about which the foremost experts on the War Against Fertility continue to disagree. Mankind has never been renowned for accepting logical solutions to its most serious problems. As a rule, the degree of logicality of solutions seemed to vary inversely with the urgency or seriousness of the problems. So when an eminently sensible solution disposed of the most serious problem of all—the threatened doubling of the world population in the latter half of the twentieth century —even the politicians could be forgiven for being a little nonplussed. To have geared oneself up for an Armageddon that never took place was a frightening thing. By the year A.D. 2000 the incidence of nervous breakdown among distinguished statesmen was about one in three. Few presidents, prime ministers, or first secretaries were eager to seek a second term of office. The fascination of power for its own sake was waning.

But while the luminaries of the international political scene were passing through an acutely depressive phase, the women of the world—or most parts of it—were basking in the high noon of emancipation. Not the phony emancipation that "freed" women from the maternal bonds imposed by men, that allowed them—with an inferior physique, a smaller brain capacity, and several thousand years of mental inhibitions—to operate on an equal-pay-for-equal-jobs basis. But the real emancipation. The emancipation from the bondage of evolution. The right to contract out as a child-bearing machine.

It went to their heads. In the West first, of course. It definitely went to their heads. The birth rate declined so rapidly that the Catholic Church had ecumenical hysterics (after trying and failing to face the facts for half a century).

8

It used up four popes in ten years and then split in two, each part thereafter subdividing at regular intervals until what had once been a great institution finally achieved a sort of slow-motion parody of that lowly creature the amoeba. Eventually, as always, the Anglican Church followed suit. Buddhism, on the other hand, seemed to be somewhat more robust and capable of accepting—in theory, at least—a new level of existence. So did Islam. But in the end both had to be modified. Drastically modified.

Meanwhile, women everywhere reveled in the emancipation from animalism. Three pregnancies—the sentence of the average married/mated human female in the earlier decades of the twentieth century—did not only mean twenty-seven months as a fetal vehicle. It meant at least thirteen years as a programmed teaching machine. It meant one quarter of the total average female life span. That was the real bondage. It was the mechanism by which maidens were turned into matrons, and matrons were turned into crones.

Birth control, practiced by the minority since the dawn of civilization, became the prerogative of the masses. It was the end of the million-year slavery. It was the beginning of woman, the social force. It was also the end—quite by accident—of man, the master.

By the early 1970's, contraception had become a major industry. The population of the world was nearly four thousand million. Therefore there were roughly two thousand million females, nearly half of whom were in the child-bearing age range. The 1970's became the Golden Age for the birth-control propagandists, the great drug houses, and the pharmaceutical chemists.

The IUCD—the intro-uterine contraceptive device—a simple plastic spiral inserted in the womb, was certainly one of the most efficient methods of birth control ever devised. Temporarily, however, it suffered an eclipse. It suffered an eclipse because, from the profit-making point of view, there just wasn't enough money in it. It could be manufactured for a penny and fitted by a trained nurse for ten shillings. It was virtually a complete answer, with minimal side

9

effects. So the advertising agencies—fortified by multi-million-pound appropriations—got to work and temporarily smashed it.

They boosted the pill. Any kind of pill that would do the job—but preferably one that had to be taken daily, so that the great drug houses could declare impressive dividends. Several misguided scientists produced pills that only needed to be taken once a month. The drug houses bought up the patents, or if they could not do that they bought up the companies that tried to manufacture and distribute the "lunar" pill. One misguided British biologist—unfortunately incorruptible—succeeded in developing a pill that needed to be taken only once a year. Oddly enough he soon died in a car accident, and coincidentally, his laboratory was simultaneously destroyed by fire. The formula disappeared. His widow, however, was generously provided for. She retired to the south of France.

Meanwhile, pills proliferated. By the 1980's there were fifty-seven different varieties. Many women, with commendable brand loyalty, stuck to the same pill throughout their child-bearing years. But there were also those who tried a sort of pill potpourri—having a vestigial compulsion, perhaps, to wash whiter than white.

Interesting things began to happen: in the U.S.A. first of all, then in Britain and Western Europe, then elsewhere. The proportion of male babies born began to decline slightly, with a corresponding increase in the proportion of female babies. At the same time the mortality rate for male children under the age of five increased a little, while the mortality rate for female children under the age of five decreased slightly.

There were other changes also. Most girl babies were quite as strong and as big as boy babies. Their cranial capacity was as large, if not larger. When they reached adolescence, it was no longer necessary to separate boys' athletics from girls' athletics. In all fields the girls could compete very well with the boys, thank you. In some fields they were definitely superior. . . . The psychologists had a ready answer, of course. The boys were beginning to feel insecure because they were noticeably outnumbered.

But the challenge was not only on a physical level. It was a woman mathematician who provided the first major modification to both the general and the special theories of relativity. It was a woman delegate who successfully steered through the U.N. Assembly the International Nuclear Disarmament Charter. It was a woman physicist who discovered the epsilon three particle.

By the beginning of the twenty-first century, throughout the world men were significantly outnumbered by an average majority of seven to five. By the beginning of the twenty-first century, women—or more accurately, the new breed of women—were on the move. Particularly in the West. Having demonstrated their equality and, in many cases, their superiority in several masculine strongholds—notably the sciences and politics—they began the great take-over bid.

They were, numerically, in an unassailable position. Physically and psychologically also, they were in an unassailable position. For, except by consent, and for the first time in a million years, they were—both in the literal and in the metaphorical sense—impregnable.

The orthodox Western concept of marriage took a beating. During the latter decades of the twentieth century the disintegration had been hastened both by easy divorce and by the more efficient and widespread birth control. With the development of greater social security and a noticeable numerical imbalance between the sexes, marriage—as a social institution—fell apart. It became socially acceptable for women to live with men as and when they wished. It became socially acceptable for women to have babies without declaring or involving the father. Promiscuity was no longer a social crime; carried to excess, it was merely regarded as slightly vulgar—rather more acceptable than gluttony and infinitely more acceptable than prudery.

Female prostitution vanished. Male prostitution began to grow. Marriage became, for the old and the rich, a status

11

symbol. For the lonely it was just a temporary refuge—a sort of friendship with the fringe benefit of instant sex.

As the twenty-first century progressed, another kind of pill came on the scene. It was a longevity pill; and though it did, in fact, slow down the aging process, it also had some peculiar side effects, such as a tendency to induce satyriasis, nymphomania, or infantile regression in certain types of individuals or in anyone who overindulged.

The longevity pill—underresearched and oversold—was a costly failure resulting, during its brief exploitation, in the damage or destruction of hundreds of thousands of individuals of both sexes. Compared to spare-part surgery—which had progressed to such a degree that practically anything except the brain and the endocrine system could be replaced—it was no more than a dangerous experiment.

It did, however, trigger off a great international effort to extend human life by artificial means. The most successful system developed consisted of a complex program of enzyme stimulation, in turn triggered by an equally complex pattern of injections, which varied according to the body chemistry of the individual. The drawbacks to the system were that it was expensive and that it had to be aligned with the psychosomatic history of each person undergoing treatment.

Inevitably, after a brief and disastrous period of exploitation by private enterprise, it passed under state control—thus providing the government with a convenient means of increasing revenue while at the same time maintaining comprehensive records of individuals. Whoever desired and could afford the longevity treatments—or time shots, as they came to be known—was at the mercy of the state. If you observed the basic rules of society and if you had an income of five thousand lions a year or more (the devalued pounds, marks and francs had long since been superseded by the European lion) your expectation of life could be extended to more than one hundred and fifty years. If you were politically or socially undesirable or if you were just plain poor, you would be denied time shots; and your expectation would be no more than ninety-five years at the most.

It was into this woman-dominated world of change that, in 2025, Dion Quern was born. He was the son of an infra —one of the steadily dwindling minority of regressive women who had no talent for anything but loving and childbearing—and a wild Irishman who had no talent for anything but alcoholism and drank himself to death a month before Dion was born.

In a society already controlled by dominas, the new type of superwomen who had demonstrated their ability to triumph against masculine opposition, Dion's mother could only earn enough money to keep him out of a state orphanage by becoming a brood mare.

So she sent him to a private nursery and retired to one of the numerous baby farms patronized by the more prosperous doms and their squires. It had become fashionable for dominas to have babies by proxy. Dion's mother became a professional proxy. It earned her two thousand lions a pregnancy and enabled her to pay for her son's progress from nursery to public school.

While he was a baby, she went to visit him regularly. When he was at public school, he went to visit her regularly. They got on well together; and despite an unhealthy real-mother—real-son relationship, they had a lasting affection for each other.

Dion rarely saw his mother when she was not pregnant. And so he came to think of her as a large, rocklike creature, whereas in fact, she had been basically small and finely formed.

She managed seventeen successful pregnancies (eleven girls and six boys) before she died of melancholia, an embolism, and a totally overloaded heart. She might have been resuscitated, of course, if she had been sufficiently important or if there had been enough lions in her bank account. But thirty-four thousand lions had been just sufficient to buy Dion an education to the point where, against stiff female competition, he won a state scholarship in cybernetics.

He never took up the scholarship. He attended the funeral, saw the oddly frail body consigned to a cleansing furnace of atomic fire, and felt the shamefully obscene tears course down his cheeks. Then he thumbed his nose at the kind of world that could do this to the only person he had ever loved, and decided to live by his wits.

He was, at the time, just eighteen years old. He had a long way to go. By the time he had matured, the ratio of men to women was five to twelve.

THREE

Dion Quern was drunk and not a little bewildered. He was drunk because he had disposed of more than half a bottle of hock before he had started on the cold chicken. He was bewildered because he was at the mercy of a big blonde Peace Officer who did not look as if she had the slightest intention of calling the dry cleaners.

Presently, with a sizable portion of cold chicken and green salad inside him, he began to feel a little better. Well enough to appreciate the brandy and the black coffee. Well enough to realize that Juno Locke was merely playing with him on a short string. When he ceased to amuse her she would let the dry cleaners cart him off to another dose of psychoanalysis.

So what? So it didn't matter a coprolite. He'd had a grade three analysis before. The psychos were further out and deeper down than the paper dolls they treated. All you had to do was toss them a few public shock images, or get all

14

twisted with submission neurosis or womb envy, and they would lay polysyllabic eggs all over the place. Then you got three decent meals a day for a month, ten shots of partial recall, fifty lions, and a year's probation. It was a bit boring, really, but not too inconvenient. Providing you didn't fracture the probation.

He tried to remember when he'd had his last grade three. He tried to remember in case the present contretemps was a breach of probation. That could be serious. Grade two analysis. Three months and the wide-screen treatment, including, maybe, the electronic twitcher. Less than idyllic . . . But he couldn't remember. The last dose *seemed* quite a long time ago. But so did yesterday's breakfast. . . .

Juno Locke sipped her brandy and coffee and read his thoughts.

"I'd say not less than six months and not more than a year. Bad luck, stripling. It could be a grade two."

He jumped as if she had put another laser hole in him. "How the Stopes do you know?"

"I've seen the look before, little one, many times. When a sport falls flat, usually the first thing that happens is the far look. He's trying to remember when he had the last analysis. He's trying to work out if he'll move up a grade. Not being able to remember is a bad sign. It's a sign of not wanting to remember. . . . Now, have some more brandy and make me laugh."

"Bulldozer!" he shouted furiously. "Sex zombie! Shrivel-womb!"

She smiled. "Please. You're bruising my ego."

"I'd prefer it to be your throat."

Juno surveyed him calmly. "You're quite a big little meistersinger, really, I suppose. Care to try?"

"Nobody is worth grade one—not even a Peace Officer."

"So," she said gaily, "at last we're getting sensible. Have some more brandy. . . ." She poured a large measure into his glass. "Let there be civility all around." She picked up a light house tunic and slipped it on, covering her breasts. "There, how's that?"

15

"Thank you," said Dion. "It seems rather fair."

"Aha, I thought you were old-fashioned."

He smiled. "Let's say just quaint. Eccentric would be an even better word."

"And you really do write poetry?"

"It has been called that, chiefly by me. I have a most appreciative readership—of one."

"Widen your horizon, then. Expand it to two."

"The time is out of joint," he said dryly.

"O cursed spite," she retorted, laughing, "that ever I was born to set it right. . . . But were *you* born to set it right? In the twenty-first century, Hamlet would rate a grade one analysis on about ten separate counts."

Dion's mouth fell open.

"Please don't be too amazed. It might offend. Not all doms are illiterate."

"Not even Peace Officers?" he managed to say.

"Especially not Peace Officers. The job is almost a sine-cure. Sports like you tend to have a built-in death wish. You dig nothing by a one-inch epitaph."

Again he was nonplussed.

"The query is," she went on, "what to do with a doomed meistersinger? Shall I keep you—or shall I let them hang you out to dry?"

"Have fun," he said, trying to sound indifferent. "It's a sweet and lovely world."

"Then I'll keep you. The horizon shall be expanded."

"How much a lay?" he demanded coldly.

"Or how much a roundelay?" she countered. "Sex before sonnets, or sonnets before sex? Perhaps even sex *and* sonnets. Orgasm, rhyme, and rhythm in a package deal. Twee, grotty, and deviant, withal."

Dion sighed and stood up—somewhat unsteadily. "Send for the cleaners, and we'll sing a duet. You're a paper doll yourself. Thank you for the brandy, chicken, and all such; and I'll bid you a very good night."

"Sit down, dimhead!"

He blinked at her and sat.

16

"Now listen carefully. I'm sixty-two and less than ugly, and that makes you twice lucky. You, I'd say, are late forties and needing time shots. You've got as much future as I care to allow. A single word, and a few cuts and bruises on each of us—less than difficult to arrange—and you're fully programmed for a grade two with a five-year denial of shots. Do I make the signals clear?"

"Loud and pellucid."

"Then keep the short-wave channel open, love, and don't make a sound like unrestrained mirth or I'll chop you in two. I'm sixty plus—in the first bloom, no less, on my aging sequence—beautiful rather than ugly, even by your depraved standards, and my credit key is good for ten thousand lions. I am also a little lonely—not too much, but a little. I have an insatiable curiosity, and I don't worry greatly about how much time I spend or don't spend with my legs apart. I like to take reasonable chances, and I think I'd like to find out what happens, if anything, inside a reconditioned meister-singer. . . . Still receiving signals?"

Dion hiccupped. "Locked on the beam."

"If you want independence, stripling, I'll buy it for you. Squire me, that's all. Sex is your problem, not mine. Scribble verse, if you wish, and stick it in a radio locker. I won't pry. All I require are civilized motions—and an absence of analyzable crime. . . . Now, drink another brandy, rattle the marbles in your head, and don't speak for two minutes."

Dion did as he was told. The marbles rattled with a most peculiar sound.

Juno Locke, Peace Officer, blonde, sixty-two, was less than scrutable. No rape, no dry cleaners, no flesh wounds—except a couple of introductory laser holes. Most interesting.

She had a nice box, no recent signs of squiredom, and a voice that was softer than many.

He yawned. "Stopes, I'm tired. It's been a nocturne plus."

Juno smiled. "Less than elegant, but it's an honest answer. Let's go to bed."

17

FOUR

The bar was called *Vive le Sport*. It was a drab little place on the Piccadilly sub-level, occupying some of the space that had been taken up about a century before by the London Pavilion dream house.

Dion had more than enough trove in his pocket to cover an evening of serious drinking—which was not his primary intention, but merely plan seven, in case the first six serendipities fell flat.

He had squired Juno for the best part of a week, not unpleasantly. Off duty, and that was most of the time, they had cavorted cautiously, observing each other's psychic profiles, noting when to hit the go button and when to reach for the abort switch. Aberrations were minimal: they matched velocities well enough.

One evening, just for repercussions, they had hovered through the tunnel to Paris simply because Dion wanted to walk by the Seine and then eat raw onions and fresh French bread. Juno was amused, but only just. Afterwards they went to one of the absolute music spots on the Champs Elyseés.

But tonight, tonight the dom was in her Peace Officer guise—or at least improving her career by personal attendance at a scholarly little conclave on Prerecognition of Deviance in Adjustment Feedback. The conclave was at the Cambridge Psycholab, and would doubtless consist of a twittering of profs and big-breasted PO's with nary a sport in sight. He wished her great joy of it.

Meanwhile, the night needed no time shots—and here

he was at the *Vive le Sport,* complete with its sun room, hourly rented bedchambers, and basement steam bath.

The bar itself was almost deserted—a long, wonderfully hideous bar of genuine twentieth-century tiles, instant-antique oak, and dull red neon tubes. There was even a century-old juke box (for ornamental purposes only) and synthetic sawdust on the floor. It was, thought Dion, as near as you could get to the age of the masculine pre-twilight.

He was, however, fascinated by the *Vive le Sport* in spite of itself and because of its bartender.

The bartender was simply called No Name—because, more often than not, he couldn't remember it. He was a fat, blank-faced man, looking just like anyone aged a hundred and seventy-three who had run out of time shots half a century before. In fact, he was exactly Dion's own age, and the last living political assassin in England. Just about ten years ago he had cut the Minister of Creative Activity in two with a laser rifle. So he had collected total recall, a grade one analysis, and suspension of time shots in perpetuity.

No Name was a celebrity and something of a hero among unattached sports. One entire wall of the bar was covered by a badly scrawled citation which described his crime and punishment and wound up by proclaiming him to be a Heroine Mother of the Soviet Union, Tenth Class. It had become a tradition of the house that sports visiting the bar for the first time should add their signatures to the citation, thus endorsing No Name's Canute-like gesture against the advancing tide of women. It wasn't that he had ever had anything personal against the previous Minister for Creative Activity (who, inevitably, now rested in the Abbey). But she had been a dom's dom, and she had been responsible for the Restrictive Employment Act. And both reasons were excellent.

According to legend, No Name had once been a slightly brilliant architect. But that, of course, was woman's work.

19

Hence the big joke with the laser rifle—and the subsequent nocturnal *après-midi* of a quasi-human monolith.

"Beer," said Dion, propping himself up at the deserted end of the bar. *"Löwenbrau* Special. Cold."

Expressionless, No Name found the bottle, selected a glass with the care a brain surgeon might take in choosing his scalpel, and poured. "One lion fifty."

Dion slapped some mobile money on the bar. "You, too?"

"Danke schön, sport. That makes three. Best goddam gnat piss. Who can afford to drink it but you, me, and slumming doms? Here's led in your pencil." Expertly, No Name downed the *Löwenbrau* in one.

The three sports at the other end of the bar unsubtly moved a little nearer. They liked the sound of the word *Löwenbrau*. Clearly the lad with largesse was a squire playing truant.

"The bestest," said one with a carrying voice, "is to sterilize all infras. It needs big battalions, of course. But it's a surefire bestseller. That way the doms drop flat."

"Square root of nix," said another, "on behalf of the human race."

"He's right, matey," said the third. "Leave us snatch selected top doms, shoot them full of contra-contra, pump a few squires full of aphrodiz to fertilize same with high speed enthusiasm, and then watch their bellies grow. Hara-kiri for top people. Haw haw."

"Switch channels," said No Name. "Crap talk. They want to ride you."

Dion surveyed the three sports. "So I've squired, jacks," he said. "So I have lions aplenty. Make an edifice of it. What shall it be—free style, karate, or kung-fu? Or *Löwenbrau* Specials for any who care to drink with the fallen?"

"Spoken like a sport," retorted the would-be sterilizer. *"Löwenbraus* five, No Name. Let there be a glad sound in Israel."

Dion emptied his glass and nodded. Fresh glasses appeared on the bar, bottlecaps whooshed, and the three sports became temporary blood brothers.

"Gents," said Dion, raising his second glass, "I give you Renaissance man."

"Renaissance man," said the three in unison.

"And you know what you can do with him," went on Dion, putting down his glass. "Because you and I, dear drinking friends, are jackals. We have outstayed our welcome. We are craven bloody cowards. We are the ultimate excreta of mankind. Because the doms made it and we didn't."

"I'll drink to that," said No Name with some enthusiasm.

Dion looked at him. "What the hell *is* your name?"

No Name scratched his head for a moment or two. "James Flamingo Bond," he said. "Now what the hell is yours?"

FIVE

Blood brotherhood waxed gaily with the frequent appearance of *Löwenbrau* Specials. The three sports, slightly built, cadaverous creatures who looked as if they might all have been extruded from the same consignment of flesh-colored plastic, were named Pando, Harvil, and Tibor. None of them was productively employed. They lived by scavenging, petty larceny, and prostitution. Despite the fact that Dion had descended to squirarachy, they magnanimously forgave him. The color of his trove was inherently beautiful.

"All we need," said Pando, disposing of his fourth, "is just one mad bad drainbrain, male. One lousy sport with some scrambling of science in his nutshell."

21

"All drainbrains are doms," protested Tibor. "You know that. Science is strictly female. No big tits, no IQED."

Pando burped. "Dinosaurs we are not, yet," he announced. "There has got to be a drainbrain somewhere—even if hiding in the sewers and operating with beer bottles and coke straws."

"So we have the drainbrain, hypotheoretically, then what?" demanded Harvil. "One drainbrain maketh not a multiplicity of sports."

Nein, non and *nyet*. One drainbrain maketh an antidom bug, a streptococktail of some perception. Both bug and manufacturer being, of course, fully programmed. Then we slip the bug in the reservoirs, casting much upon the waters, and sit back while the doms pop ballonwise and preferably with some discomfort."

"Dreams," said Dion in exasperation. "Chronomyths of the illiterate. What the Stopes would you do with the world on a silver plate? The doms will stay forever if it depends on sports droning bee features in a million drowning bars. The need is not for bugs, bombs, or bludgeons. The need is only for men. Stand up, sports. Stand three feet taller and be counted."

There was a brief silence. Finally it registered with Pando that he might possibly have been insulted. "What's with you, squire?" he sneered. "The spiel comes big from a hired holefiller. Climb a ladder and count yourself."

"Gents," said Dion patiently, "the point I make is that jackal *v.* lioness is grotty stone cold. If there were men aplenty the doms would keel in rows. *Ergo* rethink."

"Square one point five," agreed Harvil solemnly. Then, recollecting his basic loyalty, he added, "Your face affords some slight offense."

"Oh dear and lovely fellows," said No Name, coming suddenly to life, and with tears in his eyes, "I drink to the universal brotherhood of man. . . . Christ Jesus, a war party!"

Dion and the three sports followed his gaze.

Seven large and physically magnificent doms had just

22

entered the bar. They were a little grimy and carelessly dressed. Three of them wore battered fiberglass helmets.

"Irish Sea cows," whispered No Name. "The big bitches came here last week. Five hundred lions damage, and they pay from waist belts. Live gently, sports. These red hot mammals don't care like zero cubed."

"Gas?" inquired Dion, observing the doms with interest. "Oil? Minerals?"

"No. Submarine hotels and suchlike. They tell me there are doms and high-spirited squires who like to lie double and gaze up at the naughty little fishes through carbon glass."

The doms arranged themselves noisily around a table in one of the bar's semi-oubliettes. Evidently they had already had much to drink, for their actions and verbiage were larger and louder than life.

One of them, a tall and startlingly masculine brunette, slammed the table with her fist. *Vino! Vin! Vinho!*"

"Attending, dear doms." Expertly, No Name vaulted over the top of the bar and went to take their orders.

At the same time, one of the doms detached herself from the group and sauntered a trifle unsteadily over to the bar. She surveyed Dion and his companions critically.

"One for loneliness," she said, "two for companionship, three plus for conspiracy. Have at you, sports. The night needs no shots."

"No shots, indeed," said Tibor, sticking out his chest. "Have at you, dear dom, now and hereafter."

She looked him up and down, then flung five lions on the bar. "You'd never make the second round, infant. Have a glass of milk."

Tibor gazed at the lions and swallowed the jibe. "Largesse and loveliness. Let us drown what might have been in *Löwenbrau.*"

Harvil looked at the dom and tried to make his eyes smolder. "Five rounds at least," he said softly. "Genuine, vintage, bona fide, guaranteed."

The dom smiled. "Conviction and courage," she said. "A

possible combination. You are thin, but no matter. I've seen better and I've seen worse." She threw out a hand and efficiently arrested No Name on his way back to the bar to fulfill orders received. "A bedchamber, minion. Your little jack presumes to be a giant killer."

"Number three," said No Name, fishing a key from his pocket. "Seven fifty the hour."

"Oh, the high price of sin!" She turned to Harvil. "Can you last an hour, brave one?"

Harvil licked his lips. "For twenty a throw, I can last till close of play."

She laughed. "Delusions gratis. For your sake, the deeds should match the words." She took the key, threw an arm around Harvil in proprietory fashion, and called to her companions. "Sayonara, briefly, bosom friends. I go to test a little steel. Don't drink the well dry till I get back."

"In about ninety seconds," prophesied a rich contralto voice.

"Go ride yourself! At least three minutes!"

The captive and docile Harvil was led toward the bedchamber level.

No Name carried drinks across to the doms. There was a burst of laughter, then two or three of them glanced meaningly at the bar. Presently one of them—a handsome and obviously bouncy speciman—came across to the bar.

She looked at Dion. "Care to?"

"It would be a privilege, but no," he said carefully. "My fish fries elsewhere."

"It was not so much a question," the bouncy dom explained. "More of a regal invitation."

"Abjectly declined," responded Dion, "with profuse stereophonic apology."

Her voice became hard. "Jack, when I invite, only a brave sport declines."

"Felicitations. In this case a coward also declines. May I offer you a drink?"

There was a roar of derision from the watching doms.

24

"I am ugly, deformed, *persona non grata*?" demanded the bouncy dom in a hard voice.

"Not any. Eminently desirable, et cetera. But, alas, I prefer to drink."

"Fifty lions should inhibit your thirst."

"It doesn't. Please join me."

There was a sudden silence.

Surprisingly, the dom laughed. "Courtesy, it seems, is the new vice of the peons. I'll join you indeed, my courteous coward. Name the mental block."

Dion signaled to No Name. "*Löwenbrau*, twice."

The drinks appeared with some rapidity.

"*Grüs Gott,*" said Dion, raising his glass.

"*Salaam alaikum,*" responded the dom with a smile. Then she poured the *Löwenbrau* over his head. "And may God bless all who sail in her."

Dion spluttered. Everybody laughed.

While he was vainly trying to mop up the mess with a kerchief, the dom—spurred, doubtless, by general approval —took the other glass and repeated the process. His discomfort seemed to be out of all proportion to the quantity of liquid that had been poured over him.

"The quality of mercy is twice blessed," explained the dom. "It droppeth as the gentle rain from heaven."

Through a veil of *Löwenbrau*, Dion gazed at the mocking woman. The sounds of hilarity increased on all sides. Pando and Tibor were killing themselves with mirth.

"Ho, ho," said Tibor. "Stand three feet taller and be counted. How now, brown squire?"

Dion shook his head and took a deep breath. He gazed at the dom who had humiliated him and who now stood observing his discomfort with immense satisfaction.

"That," she said, "may teach you to be more of a man."

"And this," retorted Dion, striking wildly at her throat with the hard edge of his hand, "may teach you to be more of a woman."

The dom was not expecting retaliation. The chop connected with her throat, and she grunted. Dion followed the blow with a straight finger thrust to her stomach. As she doubled, he hit the back of her neck for good measure.

She fell to the floor and lay there, twitching and groaning.

"Any more for the skylark?" inquired Dion savagely. "Any number can play."

Again, briefly, there was silence. Pando and Tibor gazed at him in awe.

Then there was the sound of a chair being moved. It seemed to reverberate like thunder. One of the doms in the oubliette stood up and walked toward him. She was one of the most beautifully proportioned human beings he had ever seen. A full Negress. About six foot six, but slender and feline. Her dark, muscular arms seemed to ripple with power.

"I'm afraid," she said, in perfectly modulated English, "you have hurt my friend. That is a shade unsociable. I'm sure you must now be most unhappy."

"Get her away," said Dion, indicating the dom at his feet. "She has had too much to drink."

"Certainly," said the tall Negress. "We have all had too much to drink. But first, without prejudice and if you will allow me, I'm going to break you in two."

Out of the corner of his eye Dion saw that two of the other doms had also left the oubliette. He glanced desperately at Pando and Tibor. "Now is the time for all good men to come to the party of the first part."

"Nix," called Pando. "Retroactive resignations effective instantly. Happy touchdown, squire. Unto them that hath shall be given."

In desperation, Dion snatched a bar stool. He held it with the legs pointed toward the tall Negress. "Come one step nearer," he threatened, bracing himself against the bar, "and I'll teach you to stand on a barrel and sing God Save the Queen."

The Negress smiled and continued to advance.

With an expert movement, No Name, who was immediately behind Dion on the other side of the bar, snatched a loaded plastic truncheon apparently from nowhere and brought it down forcibly on the back of Dion's skull. The world exploded, and he fell soundlessly to the floor.

"Good night, sweet prince," said No Name gently. "The sentiment may be sublime, but a fracas is definitely bad for trade."

Everybody laughed, and drinks appeared on the bar as if by magic.

Eventually, since Dion perversely refused to return to consciousness, No Name called for an ambulance.

SIX

The domdoc looked down at him disapprovingly. "Making inflammatory statements, creating a fracas, assaulting citizens with bric-a-brac and felonious intent—you've had quite a concerto, haven't you?"

"Who neutralized me?" asked Dion, sitting up in bed too rapidly, then lying down again as the throbbing started.

"The bartender," said the domdoc, "in a moment of divine afflatus. He possibly saved you from racism, first-degree murder, and a grade one. Give the man a cigar."

"How fares the target area?" Dion felt his head gingerly. There was one hell of a bump.

"You'll live," said the domdoc despondently. "Regrettable, but someone up in orbit has an addiction for mysterious ways. . . . You're a critical mess, Dion Quern. I've checked your heart, brain, and record. You were born for a grade one; if not now, then before you run out of time-shot program."

"Get stuffed."

27

"Playback?"

"Get stuffed. It's an archaic exhortation," he explained patiently. "It suggests that the addressee should have recourse to a phallic symbol."

She frowned. "You offering?"

"With concussion and a hangover? It would be unethical."

"I see. . . . Well, my clever little sport, it depends on me whether you are recommended for treatment or not. I shall think about it—while looking for a phallic symbol."

"Squire," he corrected gently. "I've been downgraded to respectability."

She raised her eyebrows. "Who the Stopes would be so sickinky?"

"Juno Locke, Peace Officer, London Seven."

The eyebrows receded further. "Elaborate hoaxwise?"

"Sorry to disappoint. Quasi-legit. Suck it and see."

"It isn't registered."

"You're so right. Informal, recent, and definitely pro tem."

The domdoc sighed. "I'll call her and see if she wishes to claim the body. Stopes help you if negative. I wouldn't offer you squiredom if you were the last man with a Y-chromosome."

"We all have our funny little ways," conceded Dion. "For the great nonlove you bear me, please make the call."

"I'll be back," said the domdoc. "If it fits, you can be out of the hospital pronto. If it doesn't fit, we may even have to get acquainted." Surprisingly, she smiled. "Incidentally, don't try the window. It's laser linked. I'm sure you wouldn't like a nasty blister on your psyche, would you?"

"I wouldn't know," responded Dion. "There is a death wish that shapes our ends, rough-hew them how we will."

The domdoc, brightly efficient and on the right side of her century, departed from the room. She returned in a couple of minutes.

"You're so right. Juno Locke, Peace Officer, London Seven. Now will I believe in Father Green Shield."

28

SEVEN

From the balcony Juno gazed out over London. It was a warm, sunny afternoon. Half a mile below, autumn leaves were spiraling gently down to earth from colonies of semi-disrobed trees. The blue sky, though slashed with vapor trails and occasionally outraged by the dull distant crack of a strato-rocket on re-entry, was hung with a sad and tranquil blueness. To the east it was possible to see where the great snake of the Thames became lost in the bleak stretches of the North Sea.

Sitting in the comparative darkness of the room, Dion looked out through the French window at Juno. She was wearing a blue and white sari. The blue matched the sky; the white matched the vapor trails. He was intensely interested in whether it was by accident or by design.

Juno turned to him. "I talked to the Quasimodo who neutralized you at the *Vive le Sport*," she said evenly.

"No Name? I'll talk to him myself in a day or two," said Dion, touching the still large bump on his head. "We'll see whether his *a priori* argument is as good as his *a posteriori* line. The bastard wields a mean instrument of sweet reason."

"You'll let him ride," retorted Juno.

"Suppose I don't want to?"

"I'll persuade you. There can be no joy in squashing a vegetable."

"This vegetable has spikes."

"Avoid the spikes. You were an idiopath to go there in the first place."

"I love you," said Dion.

29

"Playback?"

"I love you. This grade one vegetable hits me over the memory bank, and you expect me to turn all metaphorical."

"I interviewed him officially as a Chief Peace Officer. He claims you were conspiring with three itinerant sports to do fearful injuries to all doms. He further claims you inflicted grievous bodily harm on one dom and threatened another. Assuming a forty percent truth quotient, your evening's work short-lists you for a grade two."

Dion roared with laughter. "If that's the score when I'm an innocent bystander, Stopes help me when I really go to travail."

Juno sighed. "Well, then, stripling, what is *your* story-board?"

Dion told her all that had happened. But to his surprise, she hardly appeared to be listening. The air was still, and his voice carried clearly through the open French window. But she gazed toward the horizon without a flicker of expression on her semiprofile. When he had finished, she remained silent for a while. Then she took a scrap of paper from the top fold of her sari and read from it:

> *"Windswept words of brown and bronze*
> *whisper in avenue and lane*
> *of subterranean midnight suns*
> *and broken journeys of the brain.*
>
> *Whisper of archaic lunar seas*
> *and pools of interstellar space*
> *that whirl behind the frozen mask,*
> *the stamped medallion of the face."*

Dion gazed at her appalled. Then he dashed into the bathroom, unlatched the grille over the warm-air duct and felt behind it. The antique writing pad was still there. So was the pencil. In a towering rage, he went out on to the balcony.

"You bloody great bitch! What do you do—search the box every night?"

"I'm sorry," said Juno humbly. "I'm sorry. I hoped—"

"Don't hope," he snapped savagely. "You've got enough lions to rent my body, but I'm damned if you'll ever even see enough to pay the rent for my psyche. That was no part of the bargain."

He was gratified to see a watery brightness in her eyes. Impulsively he snatched the slip of paper, tore it into tiny pieces, and scattered them over the side of the balustrade. Presently they mingled with the convoys of falling leaves.

"They were such strange and lovely words," she said softly.

"Archaic doggerel in a worn-out style."

"Lovely, regardless."

"Crap. Verbal excreta—the sick imaginings of a vagrant sport."

She turned to him. "You see, Dion, that's why I don't want you to walk into a grade two. Those kind of words will die. You know that. You must know it."

He hit her. She didn't move. The mark showed on her cheek.

He hit her again. Still she didn't move.

For several appalling seconds they stood staring at each other.

Then suddenly he put his arms around her and kissed her on the lips. It was only about the third time in his entire life, he had ever kissed a woman because he really wanted to.

Her blue sari pressed against him, her breasts pressed against him, her belly pressed against him. He was amazed that there was so much life in her body. It pulsed, it vibrated. It shivered and leaped.

He tasted salt on her lips; and the salt taste was sweet.

EIGHT

Dion sniffed the cool clean air of morning. It drifted in through the still open French window, combating the air streams from the room's heat ducts and the subtle after-scent of sexual frenzy.

He looked at Juno, her eyes still closed, still lying naked and luxuriously crumpled like a great plastic doll by his side. She was beautiful—there was no doubt about that. But then all living things were beautiful. The great trick was to stand—or lie—where the beauty was visible. . . .

Between them they had made an afternoon, an evening, and a night of it. They had made love until they were exhausted. Then they had ordered food and drink; and when it popped up through the vacuum hatch, they had carried the tray to bed and greedily energized their bodies to the point where they could face ecstasy again. So it had gone on; and now the party was over. Passion was spent, and there remained only tenderness. And much surprise.

He stroked her breasts speculatively with his knuckles. There was no response. She was inert—as any self-respecting plastic doll should be. He smiled to himself, remembering the vagaries of the night. The dom had disintegrated into sheer femininity. The Peace Officer persona had been shed like a disposable garment, revealing only the million-year-old woman who wanted, above all, to be sexually subdued.

That was something to think about. What if all doms were basically like this? But all doms weren't. There were those who were as hard as carbon steel—who had, to all intents and purposes, rejected the million-year program-

32

ming. Dion knew them well, from personal experience—bitter personal experience. So perhaps Juno was not really a dom. Perhaps she was merely an infra in disguise. That would be one hell of a bisociation. Perhaps she just wanted a riot of rides and a multiplicity of babies.

But no. Beautiful she might be; but basically she was still a shrivel-womb. Babies to her would be messy and sordid—an affront to that superb muscular body.

He got up from the bed and went across to the pick-up by the vacuum hatch.

"A large pot of tea. Eggs lightly boiled. Toast, butter, marmalade. Accoutrements for two. Ten from the time of order. Out."

Hearing his voice, Juno stirred.

"Dion, what time is it?"

"Seven-thirty—and the air sings with a music that no one will ever learn to play."

"Stopes! I'm on duty this morning. Ten-thirty."

"Rest tranquil. All mankind is on duty today and every day. . . . How are your memory circuits?"

She sat up, shook her head, and smiled. "Well enough to tell me that I love you, little meistersinger."

He sat on the edge of the bed. "Love is a four-letter word—like life. One should never be obscene before breakfast."

She laughed. "I'll give you today's epigram. It wasn't really the sexstasy."

He looked at her coolly. "It wasn't really anything but sex. . . . Sex is a clean three-letter word. Much easier to define than love."

She made a face at him. "You want to fight, stripling?"

He shook his head. "It would only gratify you. You wanted to be loved. Now you want to be hurt."

"It's no use, Dion. I'm not going to quarrel with you today."

"Such is the prerogative of the ruling sex. Whoever pays the pauper calls the tune."

She hit him with a pillow. Then breakfast arrived. They ate it sitting together on the bed, naked and relaxed.

"How would you like to make it formal?" asked Juno presently.

"Make what formal?"

"Squiredom."

He shrugged. "It matters not. What do you want to do— put a brand mark on my forehead? Or will you equip me with a bell so that I may parade the streets, uttering loud cries of 'Unclean!'"

"I'm not going to quarrel with you today."

"Then make it formal, if you wish—to celebrate the one day on which we are destined not to quarrel."

She laughed and jumped up from the bed. "Deviant to the last—that's my little troubadour. I'll call the Registrar General before you switch channels in your mazy-dazy mind."

"Not like that," said Dion, taking the breakfast tray back to the vacuum hatch.

"Breasts covered?"

"Breasts covered. I'm a reactionary fascist beast."

Juno went to the masterboard and pressed two buttons. The bed shot back into the wall and another section of wall slid to one side, revealing a profusion of clothes.

Dion went to the bathroom and turned on the shower. "Purify yourself first, you big bitch," he called. "It's not every day you put a ring through the nose of a poet."

She followed him into the bathroom, and together they stood under the shower. Dion looked at her through the needle-sharp jets of water. The bright blonde harvest of hair lay flattened now to her head, giving her face an oddly boyish look. Juno seemed to be almost exactly his own height, yet she frequently called him little. Remembering this, he gripped her hair fiercely and jerked her head back. He bent a little and twisted, letting his teeth lie on her exposed throat.

Her breasts were pressed against him. Such proud and confident breasts. Briefly, he hated them. When he took his mouth away from her throat there were two semicircles of red marks. The sight gave him some satisfaction.

34

Juno stared at him. "How strange. I find it hard to believe that I would ever let any man do that to me." The rivulets of water ran down her surprised face, turning it into a thing of beauty.

Dion laughed. "Don't measure the tiger by its tail, Peace Officer. Now let us formalize my prostitution."

Juno blew her hair, and put on a plain gold bathrobe. Dion wound a towel around him like a loincloth. They went back into the living room and stood before the plate. Juno dialed.

"Registrar General's office. May I assist?" The face was that of a vaguely Eurasian woman. She wore the routine mauve tunic of the Civil Service.

"I—that is, we—wish to register a squiredom," said Juno.

"Stand by, please, for registration."

The screen clouded; then a rather old face appeared, still female. This one was on the wrong side of her century, thought Dion. She wore a loose black vest.

"Registration squiredom," she said severely.

"My name is Juno Locke. JLF, 23A, 27C. I wish to enter an unlimited time contract with Dion Quern."

"Identity number?"

"DQM, 17L, 85B," said Dion. "Mole on left testicle and compulsive producer of doggerel."

"Playback?" said the registrar.

"DQM, 17L, 85B," said Juno hastily.

Black Vest dialed and pressed a couple of buttons out of the range of vision. There was a short pause, then she said, "The subject is a behavior problem. DQM, 17L, 85B has already received three grade-three analyses. Further deviance could result in a grade two program."

"I know that," said Juno.

"I see." Black Vest appeared to disapprove of the knowledge. "Do you require mortality benefits?"

"Yes."

"Then you will both step closer to the plate, please. . . . Do you, Juno Locke, being free of coercion or any unlawful pressure, offer a squiredom contract of unlimited duration to Dion Quern?"

"I do."

"And do you, Dion Quern, being free of coercion or any unlawful pressure, accept this contract of squiredom for unlimited duration?"

"In sickness and psychosis."

"Playback?"

Juno surreptitiously trod on his toes. "I do."

"Then, Juno Locke, kindly insert your right thumb in the scan ring."

Juno held her thumb for a second against the tiny screen under the main plate, so that its loops and whorls could be checked against her number and a facsimile of the print attached to the contract.

"Now, Dion Quern, please place your right thumb in the scan ring."

When he had done so, Black Vest said, "The contract has now been entered. Do you have any further transaction?"

"No, thank you," said Juno.

Black Vest rewarded her with a frozen smile. "Good morning and out." The screen went dark.

"Happy birthday," said Dion. "How does it feel to have an instant gigolo?"

"As before. Apart from the mortality clauses, the only difference is that you can inherit my untold trove and I can demand a baby."

"Would you bear it yourself?"

Her face clouded. "Reprogram, stripling. I don't indulge in farmyard fun."

"Afraid of offending that trim golden belly?" he inquired with malice. "According to legend, if you breast-feed, the muscles all go back. On the other hand, the breasts get slack. Nature is a shade careless, don't you think?"

She flung herself at him fiercely and gripped his body with sudden strength. "Don't be too humorous, meistersinger," she hissed. "The words leave a bad taste."

36

"A worse taste than you think, shrivel-womb," he retorted calmly. "My mother—a *real* mother: I told you I was eccentric—died after seventeen pregnancies. That was the price of my education. Seventeen infants, seventeen pans of afterbirth and one embolism. So I'm an authority on reproduction. I can tell you all about toxemia, induction, prolapse, torn vagina, mastitis, post-natal depression. That was her world; and as she was running out of time, I had to find out about it, to know what she was enduring for my sake . . . Have you ever seen a baby's head crowning? Have you ever seen the new wrinkled skull, the matted tufts of hair, the flecks of blood, the thin halo of steam? Have you ever sniffed that sweet, overpowering scent of birth?"

Juno fled to the bathroom, retching.

NINE

Dion walked down the Strand ped-level, singing. No one noticed; no one cared. In fact there was hardly anyone to do either, for it was seven o'clock on a fine October morning and the gray veil of dawn was just conceding to the harsher light of day.

It was two weeks since he and Juno had entered into an unlimited time contract, and he was beginning to recover from the indignity. The credit key that she had given him burned in his reticule like a slug of radioactive isotope. But he needed it. He needed it to pay for the time shots.

Idly, he had even considered using it to bankrupt her account. Ten thousand lions, she had said. That would be enough to take him to Bogota or Samarkand, to let him live in luxury for a couple of years before operating on some other unsuspecting dom.

But something stopped him. Loyalty? No. Love? No. Pride? Possibly . . . Pride, he reflected, was about the only thing he couldn't sell.

Also, he resented the fact that Juno trusted him. She had no right to trust him. It was presuming upon an intimacy that was simple and straightforward.

But these were hypotheoretical considerations. The immediate and practical consideration was time shots.

He had had fits of trembling. Always a bad sign. He had also begun to break out in cold sweats. And that made the matter urgent.

Longevity treatment was addictive, regardless of what the drainbrains said. Once you embarked on the program you were stuck with it—until your lions ran out and they trolleyed you off to a sweet little dodecahedronal cell.

So here he was, singing to keep the shakes off, and blasting his way footwise to the Trafalgar Square Clinic. Meanwhile, the dom was sleeping—after partaking of enough Chianti to silence the Italian Embassy, and three generous, five-star, chateau-bottled rapes.

He could, of course, have gone to the clinic in London Seven. You could get any Stopesridden thing in any of the London towers. But Dion, as always, preferred the hard way. And the hard way consisted of getting up before dawn, ignoring all modcons, and pursuing the penitents' path to Trafalgar Square.

The clinic stood where once a church called St. Martin in the Fields had stood. The church had been blown to glory in the abortive and ill-timed coup by the Sex Equality Party in '47. Three hundred desperate men had held St. Martin in the Fields and the National Gallery against the Brigade of Guards for four days. The National Gallery had contained too many priceless paintings for the Guards to risk taking it by storm; so they concentrated on making an example of the occupants of St. Martin in the Fields, which was, after all, only a church. But the defenders were surprisingly tough and surprisingly desperate. No quarter was asked or given. After a time the women of the Brigade of Guards got tired of counting their dead. They persuaded the Home Secretary to authorize the use of tactical atomics and disposed of the problem with one shell from a two-point-five mortar placed in St. James's Park. When the occupants of the National Gallery saw what had happened to their comrades, they surrendered.

By that time, the women of the Brigade of Guards were in no mood to accede to the conventions of war. Those rebels who survived the subsequent rapefest (less than fifty per cent) were removed for grade one analysis. Since that time there had been no other serious rebellions. The Brigade of Guards could hardly have found a better method *pour encourager les autres.*

Dion gazed at the clinic and thought briefly of the men who had died. He had been twenty-two when the rebellion started and, in a surge of idealism, had just joined the Sex Equality Party. As he clearly knew nothing about anything, he merely received a suspended grade three—and a maternal lecture from an elderly juridical dom whose obvious aim was to take him back to her box and feed him chocolate creams.

He looked at the titanium and carbon glass monstrosity that was the clinic and reflected vaguely on the irony of existence. Men had died on this site for a concept of freedom, and the church that had been symbolic of an immortality hereafter had been replaced by a temple of instant immortality (or at least semi-immortality) for the here and now.

He smiled, went up the pseudo-marble steps, and opened the door. The clinic's lounge was almost deserted. A trio of doms—night-hawks by the look of them—sat moodily at the bar, sipping coffee until their schedules were ready. A couple of sports lounged in contour chairs by the picture window, their attitudes and lethargy suggesting that they had slept all night at the clinic, having nowhere else to go. And a sad, wizened little woman—clearly an infra—followed

39

an electronic refuse cat as it sniffed its way about noiselessly over the floor, lapping up dust and the miniscule accretions of time.

The dom receptionist, a big bored Indian, lounged in a glass pulpit that was a replica of the one that had once stood in the erased church. The designers of the clinic had not been above sentiment—or humor. They thought it appropriate to incorporate some reminder of an institution where there had been preached a somewhat different gospel of eternal life.

Dion approached the pulpit and attempted to claim the attention of the Indian. She affected not to see him. He coughed. Still she affected not to see him. Finally he kicked the pulpit and pulled a face at her.

With an effort, she turned her head and focused, looking vaguely like one emerging from an old-fashioned LSD kick. The effort of returning to a lower and more sordid plane appeared to disgust her intently. The disgust concentrated on Dion.

"Well, insect?"

"Felicitations to Shiva," he retorted pleasantly, "and I wish to register for time shots."

"Name and ID?"

"Dion Quern, DQM, 17L, 85B."

"Cash or credit key?"

"Credit key."

"Check it, little one." She indicated the check slot on the pulpit's side. "You wouldn't accidentally con a treatment, would you?"

Dion inserted the key as requested and waited patiently for the dom to read off the balance on her meter.

"Ah, so," she said, somewhat surprised. "Thirty-five thousand plus. How doth the busy bee."

"Ah, so," echoed Dion, trying not to sound surprised. "Quite moderate, honeywise."

The dom condescended to smile. "*Scusa.* One has apprehensions. There are those, you see, who would take treatment without trove."

"It is a wicked world," he agreed, "with corruption all around us."

A tiny bell rang, and the small reception console mounted on the edge of the pulpit ejected a thin piece of plastic containing all the encoded data of Dion's psychosomatic profile. The Indian gave it to him. "Please insert your key in the debit slot. The rate is now seven see fifty."

Dion put the key in and twisted, contemplating with less satisfaction than he had expected the dent that seven hundred and fifty lions would make in Juno's credit. Ten thousand, she had said. Thirty-five thousand in fact. By damn, the big bitch was topheavy with trove.

"Drape yourself, monsieur," said the Indian, vaguely indicating the lounge with a wave of her shapely arm. "There's a good time coming."

"How long?"

She shrugged. "*Quien sabe*. It takes a while to formulate your shot bombs. Have a coffee or a pot of tea until you are called. Contemplate the infinite. Coffee, tea, and infinity are on the house."

Dion took himself to one of the contour chairs by the extraordinarily large picture window. The sports and the night-hawks ignored him, lost in their private limbos. He listened for a while to the squawk bug in the headrest of his chair, flipping his way through station after station. But after he had heard fragments of the "Marche Militaire," the absolute version of "Largo," and "Dom, dom, take me, the black kick is coming," plus fragments of verbiage in French, German, English, and Europarl, he silenced the bug with a briefly increased pressure of his head. The shakes and sweats were on him again, and he stared moodily through the window. Trafalgar Square looked like a great, vacant stadium.

Where in Stopes was that mythic band of gladiators who were dedicated to death and saluted proudly before each bloody orgasm? Where now were all the killers and the slain in this dom-ridden psychotically balanced limbo of nonlife, nondeath? Where, oh where was the once-fierce joy of living?

No answer to questions such. No, none indeed.

And yet, as he looked, a message came twisting and turning down from the gray morning sky.

It was dreamily slow. He had time for speculation, time in the heightened seconds before impact to determine the sex of the falling body. It was a dom—smooth and graceful as a seal in the standard black one-piece of the jet flipper.

He looked for the jet pack on her back. It wasn't there. He looked for the chute that should have saved her if the jets died. That too wasn't there.

So she must have jetted up over London and deliberately stepped out of the harness to enjoy her last long dance down the sky.

He had time enough to see that she was indeed dancing.

The dance of death.

Her body hit silently, close by the fountain, scattering a thousand pigeons.

Nobody noticed. Except Dion Quern.

Nobody noticed the dying fall, the cloudy ovation of the birds, the pulped protoplasm on a bed of stone. It was too early to notice such things.

A muted bell tinkled somewhere in the upholstery of Dion's contour chair, and the voice of the Indian dom said quietly, "DQM, 17L, 85B. Please attend room nine, corridor A. Your formula is ready to shoot. . . . Happy landing, squire."

Dion stood up, still gazing through the window. No doubt a Peace Officer or a passerby would shortly spot the debris and arrange for its removal.

"Send not to know for whom the bell tinkles," he murmured. "It tinkles incessantly, dear love, for thee and me."

He turned toward corridor A, unaware that his face was wet with tears.

42

TEN

The time bombs were set out in neat little rows on a trolley. They were plastic and color-coded. They looked like surrealist seashells.

The nurse was a male, possibly around Dion's own age, give or take a decade. One never knew with time shots.

"Dion Quern?"

"Himself."

"Drape your dear body, friend." The nurse indicated a wall bunk. "Strip and drape. Pushing back the clock is a wearisome business."

Dion stepped out of his tunic and lay down.

The nurse yawned. "Ho hum. Where is your data plate?"

Dion indicated the trolley on which he had placed the thin piece of plastic given him by the Indian receptionist. "I dropped it by the seashells . . . So men are still allowed to work here, then?"

The nurse gave him a thin smile. "I squire the club's top domdoc, Diogenes. For which, as a special treat, I am allowed to extend the purgatory of others." He picked up the data plate, dropped it into the slot of a small decoder built into the wall, and examined the information. He made a disapproving noise with his tongue. "Three threes. You have been a naughty boy. Next time it will be a two."

"If there's a next time," said Dion.

"There's always a next time. Now let's start you off with the base shots and dispose of the shakes."

"I'm not shaking," said Dion.

"You have been. You will be."

The nurse selected five green time bombs, deftly taped one to each of Dion's legs, one to each of his arms, and the remaining one on his chest above the heart. "My name is Smith, a fact which so far may fail to interest you. I am Leander of that fraternity. You ought to know who to curse when you collect your grade one."

"Don't confuse me," complained Dion irritably. "I've just seen a dom fall out of the sky, and I am in no mood for quippery. So program the needles, and plug the hole in your head."

Leander Smith smiled. "Rest tranquil, Dion, *mon ami*. You may wish to volunteer your sanity away——in which case you will doubtless require to glance at the scoreboard. . . . Do you enjoy living in this great domdoctored world?"

"Not wildly."

"Do you ever feel that you too could make some mild contribution to human regress—providing your life wasn't being sucked out of you by big-breasted bitches with high I.Q.'s, wide appetites, low morals, and a monopoly of lions?"

"Shove it and start the time shots." Dion was feeling oddly tired.

"I stand reproved." Leander Smith pressed a stud, and a control console shot out of the wall behind Dion's head. He heard the sound of switches being thrown, then almost immediately became aware of a brief stinging sensation in his left leg. It was followed by a similar feeling in his right leg, both arms, and finally the chest.

Meanwhile, Leander Smith was taping a series of yellow capsules to various parts of his body. As he worked, he talked.

"I'm Mephistopheles, Dion. Some bastard sport up there sent me to tempt you. Don't think of funny ploys, for Stopes' sake. The room is not wired for playback; and if it were, I'd have more to lose than you."

The euphoria—always attendant on the first shots—was beginning to take effect.

44

"What delirious drivel are you expounding?" he demanded drunkenly.

"Rebellion," said Leander. "Sexual anarchy. Universal suffrage for men. Motherhood for doms, and all manner of obscenities. You name it, I'm for it—along with a few other maladjusted psychos. Live now, take your grade one later. Want to join? It's a real fun thing."

Dion lay on the wall bunk, naked, with green and yellow time bombs taped all over him and watched Leander reset the radio trigger on the control console. Once again the pricking and tingling sensations started. He felt decidedly drunk.

"Are you—hic—pumping me full of Happyland?" he asked suspiciously.

"I cannot tell a lie. Yes, dear friend of my youth, along with the time shots I am pumping you full of Happyland. It's easier that way."

"Jackass, joker," mumbled Dion. "I'll smash your smug, smirking face."

"Try it," advised Leander. "All things are possible in this best of all possible nightmares."

Dion tried to stand up. The room began to spin and he fell back. "Buffoon," he murmured weakly, "bastard, bungling buffoon. Wait till I—wait—wait . . ." He began to giggle.

Unperturbed, Leander continued to strap the blue sequence of time bombs to his body.

"Listen, hophead. I'll straighten you out when I've had my speak. Meanwhile let the words filter through the sewage between your ears. You've already had three grade threes, so you are clearly not the goodest of good fairies. You pine a little, you live longer, and you die a lot. Put the dying to some use, friend. Join the Lost Legion. We guarantee to fix it so you can transport a few doms with you."

Dion hiccupped. "Lost Legion. Lusty Lost Legion . . . What jaded jape is this, dear Judas?"

Leander was amused. "This alliterative syndrome is a nice new quirk, laddie. But don't let it fuzz your thinking.

45

The Lost Legion I will paraphrase. Call it Male Minorities Anonymous. It's a rose by any other *nom de guerre*. Just a bunch of bright lads who are out to bust the big busts or bust themselves busting. Do I make myself clear?"

"Pel—pellucid . . . Down with the doms and up yours."

"That's it—in a nutshell. Want to play?"

"Where do I sign?"

"You don't—and *we'll* call you. Sometime. This is one Stopes of a way of recruiting." He went to the control and triggered the blue bombs. Dion felt as if his limbs, independent of his trunk, were dancing a variety of out-of-phase fandangos. The trunk was merely oscillating—like a snake with cramp.

"The thing is," went on Leander, "we're guerillas. We have to be. Not enough of us for a real stand-up-and-spit party."

"Baboons," corrected Dion blearily.

"No, just anthropoid guerillas with delusions of manhood. Where do you live, guerilla?"

"In a cage called London Seven."

"Who do you squire?"

"Juno Locke, the arid Amazon."

"What is she?"

"Peace Officer to female monkeys and frightened flunkeys."

"What an acquisition! And for Stopes' sake stop alliterizing. It's not the Happyland. There is no Happyland. It's the cockeyed euphoria."

"Cockeyed Euphoria, I love you," said Dion solemnly.

"Zip it, blabbertrap," said Leander, taping on the red bombs, the last sequence of the time shots. "This final salvo is going to sober you somewhat." He went to the console and triggered all the red bombs simultaneously.

Dion moaned, shuddered, and fainted.

By the time he came round, all the gaily colored shells had been removed and Leander was rubbing him down with some colorless fluid that burned, cooled, soothed, and invigorated all at the same time.

46

"So I lived through it," said Dion unsteadily.

"Maybe. Do you remember it?"

They looked at each other. With a shout of rage, Dion leaped off the wall bunk, his arm raised, his fist feeling like the hammer of Thor. And fell flat on his face.

Leander turned him over gently with his foot. "I forgot to tell you. Don't make any sudden movements for a while . . . Do you remember it?"

"Yes, bastard."

"Don't forget it, then. You are hereby elected to the suicide squadron. One of these dark nights you'll get a call. Take a short sharp shot and do what the voice says."

"I could denounce you to the doms."

"Joke. You've got three threes. I've got nothing. My story is the same as yours—except that my first person doesn't have a psycho record. Who wins?"

"Bastard."

"You said that before. Now let us decently cover the flesh that drives all doms to sextasy." He helped Dion up. "I think you're steady enough to walk, laddie. But remember—you're now a latent guerilla. You may not get a call till next week. You may not get one—if you're lucky—till next year. But when you get one, you operate at Mach five. And remember also—guerillas sometimes bleed."

"Cut the drama. I'm trying very hard to believe you believe it yourself."

"Try harder, Dion. Otherwise you could die laughing—hysterically."

Dion fingered the credit key in his reticule. Thirty-five thousand, less seven see fifty. It gave him a great sense of well being. And security.

He could hop to Bogota or Samarkand and sit tight till all the Leanders in London collected their grade ones and the moon jumped over all the cows who ran this great big cud-chewing world.

Then he thought of Juno with sudden senseless affection. She trusted him with the trove. Stupid bitch.

"One question."

47

"Well, Master Dion?"

"You squire a domdoc. How do you feel about her?"

Leander laughed. "You squire a Peace Officer. How do you feel about her?"

"That's no answer."

"It wasn't much of a question. Listen, Dion, a dom is just a face in the crowd. And the crowd is too damn loud and crowded. Weaken for one and you weaken for all."

Dion smiled. "Now that we're down to slogans I'll bid you a very good morning. Forever."

Leander opened the door. "Don't be afraid you'll miss the second part of the show. Forever is shorter than you think."

ELEVEN

After a night of mild lesbian frolics and occasional heterosexual interludes, the ambassadors of the United States of North and South America, the Neo-Soviet Union, and the Sino-Indian Empire, together with the Proconsul of the Grand Federation of Europe and Queen Victoria the Second, sat soberly in the private suite at New Buck House taking their morning coffee and energy rolls.

Victoria, still a fine-looking dom in her late eighties, was bored. She was bored with the routines of monarchy, the routines of state, the sports and infras of the bed chamber, the prospect of another sixty glorious years, and especially with the fragments of protocol that still clung tenaciously to her existence like cobwebs from the Dark Ages.

"Darlings," she said, quaintly affecting the novelese of

48

the late twentieth century, now once again coming into fashion, "what the hell?"

"Sweet, is that a statement or a question?" asked the Neo-Soviet ambassador. Anastasia was a wide-eyed, black-haired, breathtakingly bouncy thing on the juvenile side of fifty. She subscribed to the quite disarming and simple philosophy that politics are love—and consequently devoted all of her extrasexual energies to arranging treaties with everybody.

"Both," said Victoria. "I'm bored. In the doldrums. Life is a Möbius strip."

"Your Majesty," said Eleanor, "how about dinner at the White House? You haven't been to Brasília since the President's coronation. Besides," she added significantly, "they serve the most excellent caramel dessert."

Victoria shook her head. "We are not amused." Then, recalling that the American ambassador was a very sensitive dom, she added placatingly: "Sorry, love. I know it's the greatest show on earth, but I'm just not in the phase for big hellos. Also I don't go a megaton on having my arm shaken off and my hand kissed to the bone before the booze-up starts. I hope Sammy wasn't expecting me?"

"No, Your Majesty. But the Queen's suite is permanently ready, and the President has asked me to renew her standing invitation. You could always make it an incognito."

Victoria laughed grimly. "I had an American incognito about fifteen years ago. It rained Daughters of the Restoration, Maidens of the Plains, and the Hollywood State Choir. Don't think I don't like that sort of thing, Eleanor. It's all a question of phase."

Josephine, Proconsul of the Grand Federation, scratched her legs (thus calling attention to what a scribbling sport had once defined as France's greatest assets,) poured some more coffee, and yawned. "You are righter than right, *chérie*. It is all a question of mood. And on this last day of October I am in the mood for a new mood. Something different is required. . . . Quaint, perhaps, but different."

The ambassador of the Sino-Indian Empire suddenly

49

had an idea. "I have it, Vicky," she said. "Let me call home and get them to freeze the waters below the Taj Mahal. Then we can jet over late this afternoon, electro-roast an ox and have an olde English skating party complete with paper lanterns, Johann Strauss, and half a regiment of big virile Pathans."

"Darling Indira," said the Queen gently, "you read too much. Also we had an Indian evening—or was it an Indonesian evening?—about ten days ago. But somewhere . . . somewhere there is the virus of an idea." She turned once more to the Federation Proconsul. "What day did you say it was, love?"

"The last day of October."

"Ahah," exclaimed Victoria triumphantly. "Ace, king, queen, jack. Halloween! I knew there was something at the back of my libido. Olde Anglican custom. We'll have a witches' sabbath."

"Joy—squared and cubed," said Eleanor.

"Halloween?" inquired Anastasia dubiously.

"Halloween," confirmed the Queen emphatically. "The Eve of All Hallows, when sports go bump in the night. We'll have witches and warlocks and demons and devils. We'll have skeletons and virgins and fireworks and black magic." Then, as an afterthought, she added, "We will also have the Commons, the Diplomatic Corps, the Peace Corps, and senior civil servants. The A list, I think. The Bs are too bloody stodgy for words. . . . And everyone is commanded to arrive by jet pack and broomstick! Ha, that should be a bright little kick—particularly if we lace the booze." She patted Anastasia on the arm. "Be a dearie, and hit the go button. You're nearest. We'd better program the serfs to lay on something special."

Anastasia rang for the private secretary.

Indira, still saddened a little by the royal rejection of the Taj Mahal, said somewhat petulantly, "But where can one hold this—this witches' sabbath?"

Victoria grinned. "Where else but Stonehenge, you beautiful brown beast?"

TWELVE

At the end of the world, wrote Dion,
the sky stole blood from a rose.

He gazed hypnotically at the ancient writing pad, chewed the end of his century-old pencil for a moment or two, then reached absently for the bottle of vodka. He didn't bother to pour any. He just raised the neck of the bottle to his lips and drank.

Presently he hiccupped. Then he began to write once more:

And where darkness grows
in the hollow light of twilight,
a white island lay,
scarlike in darkness.
There was left no sensation,
only the heaving stillness
of nights' last sickness.
Continents flickered;
silent seabeds spoke
in a forked-flame play
and a mime of forgotten birds.

There was another long pause, and further consultation with the vodka. At last he received enlightenment, and the pencil whispered quickly across the page.

Wind, the smothered wind heard
too much of a tale for the keeping;
wept and swept from the planet,
as only the dying hurry
to canyon or cave or valley
where no light grows.

51

Finally, as an afterthought, he added: *Dion Quern, October 31, 2071*. Then he threw the pencil down and reached for the vodka.

Juno was sitting at the chessboard, plugged in to a game with the domestic computer of London Seven. It lived two humdred and fourteen floors below in the basement of the tower and was simultaneously playing two hundred and forty-seven games of plane chess, five games of tri-di chess, eighteen games of Go, and nine games of Hokusan. It was also programming the air conditioning, the high-speed lifts, the restaurant service and room service, and delivering its daily report to the Greater London Computer on water-and-power intake.

Juno had just typed her seventeenth move. She was two pawns down, and the computer would probably mate—as usual—before the twenty-fifth move.

She saw that Dion had finished writing.

"How goes it, love?"

"Ferkinorrible."

"What were you writing?"

"I don't know."

"You don't know?"

"If you want a label," he said irritably, "let's call it 'Footnote to a Monograph on the Possible Aftereffects of Armageddon.'"

The computer replied to the move as Juno had expected it would, and the R5 square on her chessboard glowed where the computer had just eliminated her bishop with its knight. She took the knight with a pawn and some resignation. The computer had its rooks doubled.

Juno turned to Dion once more. "There will be no Armageddon," she said confidently. "Because the affairs of the world are now virtually controlled by women."

"You stupid big-breasted bitch."

Juno stood up. As an afterthought she signaled her resignation to the computer. Then she faced Dion, arms akimbo.

"Don't mix it with me, little troubadour. Otherwise, I may have to snap you in two."

"Stupid big-breasted bitch," he repeated calmly. "What the Stopes do you know about anything, you arrogant cow?"

"You're trying to needle me."

"Ah, the dawn of intelligence in the master sex . . . No Armageddon, quoth the dom. And lo, the *pronunciamento* becomes graven on a stone tablet. Armageddon arrived some time ago, dear dim playmate. It started with a Hollywood musical called Hiroshima and worked up to a genetic climax with the usurpation of the human female." He hiccupped once more. "People got burned at Hiroshima, but by Stopes the rest of us got fresh-frozen when you shrivelwombs became pill-happy."

"I think I should order some coffee," retorted Juno with dignity.

"Do that thing. It indicates the limit of your imagination."

Juno lost her temper. She lunged across the room. Dion met her with what he hoped would be a devastating blow to the solar plexus. It never arrived. Juno snatched at his arm, translated the movement into a whip, and side-stepped. He somersaulted over the bed.

"Try again, playboy," she taunted.

With an angry growl he leaped back across the bed. Juno hit him once. He fell, retching.

"Little one," she murmured, cradling his head. "Oh, my little lost one. What is it?"

"Life," he said when he could breathe freely. "Life and vodka. Poetry and lack of hope . . . I'm sorry, shrivelwomb. This one is on me."

"Read me your poem—please."

"There isn't enough time. Kismet, via the royal command, calls us to Stonehenge."

"Victoria can wait. Besides, I doubt if we shall be presented. I'm only a second grade. Read me the poem."

Dion took the piece of paper. "You won't like it."

"Read it—please."

"You won't understand it. I'm damned if I do."

"Read it."

When he had finished, he was amazed to see that Juno was crying. There were no sounds, but the tears flowed freely down her face.

"What is it?" he asked. "Surely not recognition of genius at my time of disintegration."

"Love me," pleaded Juno. "For Stopes' sake, love me. . . . It's the damned ticking of the clock."

Dion shook his head. "Start learning, Amazon," he said. "I'll do it in my time—not in yours."

THIRTEEN

From an altitude of five hundred feet, Stonehenge looked like the wreckage of some monstrous Christmas cake. The whole area was covered by a high transparent tepee through the top of which the smoke from a butane-fed bonfire and a hundred torches rose like a solid column in the still air. The megaliths were covered with sheets of iridescent metal foil pressed hard against their contours so that metal and stone seemed as one. In the great circle, witches and warlocks seethed like a colony of disturbed ants. Victoria had evidently not yet arrived, for the royal standard was nowhere to be seen.

Dion and Juno were riding separate broomsticks. Their night sky suits glowed dully green against the star-pricked darkness. Juno's witch hat tilted precariously on the back of her head, held in position only by the band from her headlight.

The jet packs whistled softly behind the two of them as

they slowly circled the area. They dipped their headlights so that they would not blind other guests.

"What do you think?" shouted Juno against the whistle of the jets.

"I don't think," returned Dion. "Thinking is bad medicine." He glanced up. "I'll race you to the stars."

She laughed. "Not tonight, stripling. The Queen commands us."

"Coward, flatbelly, sycophant," he called. "Follow me." He switched off his headlight and opened the vertical jet throttle wide. He fell upward like a crazy stone.

Juno called, "Dion!" But he was already away, a hundred feet above her. She switched off her own light and followed him.

They both fell giddily, insanely, toward the dancing stars.

At one thousand feet the chill and rushing air made their faces tingle.

At two thousand feet frost formed on their eyebrows.

At three thousand feet they were level once more.

"Stabilize!" gasped Juno. "For Stopes' sake, stabilize." The words hurt as the freezing air ripped into her lungs.

But Dion would not or could not hear. On and upward he fell, the rush of air singing louder than the straining jets.

At eight thousand feet Juno could go no higher. The pain in her ears, the numbness in her face, the frost on her sky suit, and the deeply penetrating cold that sank through the rubber into her limbs—all these told her that she could go no higher.

"Stabilize!" she mouthed vainly. "Stabilize!" But the words had no substance, the air was too thin, and Dion had already left her behind—a sad little, mad little troubadour bent on falling upward to his fresh-frozen death at the threshold of the stars.

Juno tried to hold it at eight thousand feet. But she could not. The cold was too intense and the air was too thin. With a despairing upward glance at the shrinking speck of luminous green, she lowered slowly to five thousand feet and waited.

Dion was drunk with pain and ecstasy. His wrist altimeter showed nine thousand five hundred feet. He could hardly feel his hands; but he didn't care. The blood that had begun to flow from his nose froze on his lips; but he didn't care.

The stars were dancing. And the dance was such that a man might aspire to join.

He held for a while at ten thousand feet. Indeed, he had to, for the jet pack had a built-in pressure safety device and would take him no higher. In the past too many people had jetted up to the high reaches until the atmosphere became so thin that they lost consciousness. For a decade it had been one of the favored forms of suicide.

So he remained poised at ten thousand feet, watching the stars dance gently as the servo-jets rhythmically trimmed his attitude to the vertical. He let the cold eat through his sky suit, probing flesh and bone until it seemed to reach the very core of his personality.

The pain—the dull dead stinging of blood and nerves that were trying hard not to freeze—pleased him. He was purging himself by cold. He was confessing to the void, receiving absolution from the stars, demanding a sacrament from the great black deeps of space.

His face became a stiff mask. White crystals proliferated all over him, building a shell of ice. But still his eyes burned, translating the starlight into reflected fire.

And presently there came a satisfying sleepiness. He knew it was dangerous and played with the danger, skating deliciously along the edge of oblivion. Then vaguely, with no great feeling of urgency, he remembered Juno. A dom of great sense—and nonsense. A column of warm and pliant flesh several thousand feet below. He realized that, for no reasonable reason, he wanted her. Now. In his time. If only to savor the knowledge that he had been where she dared not follow . . . If only to see the look in her eyes. . . .

Poor, proud little dom. Magnificent of body but small of

56

spirit. No talent for dying. Only a certain comfortable talent for living. He tried to smile, but there was a smile already frozen on his face.

The stars briefly extinguished themselves—a first and dreadful warning. He groped through the darkness that was now darker than night for the jet control. He found it, but he couldn't hold it. He could only tap it feebly. It was enough.

He began to fall back through the sky, the rush of air cutting his face and body as if he were falling into a fountain of knives. At seven thousand feet his voice returned and he could scream, creating a high column of sound that rode wildly down the night.

It was a scream of pain and pleasure. For the pain gave pleasure as feeling tore back into his body, the unendurable agony of resurrection.

He passed the five thousand level, where Juno cruised frantically, waiting for him. Searching the sky, she saw his downward track against the Milky Way and jetted toward him, switching her headlight on and signaling frantically.

He didn't notice her. He was hypnotized now by the fiery circle of Stonehenge rushing up through the cosmos as if eager to touch him. How delightful to dive clean into that tiny central point that was the bonfire and send a shower of sparks and scattered life force over all the guests who were celebrating idiocy in the age of idiocy.

But at one thousand feet he decided to forego the pleasure. There was yet, perhaps, some living to be done. There was yet, perhaps, some purpose to be found—even if only a more artistic way of dying.

He hit the control once more and retro-jetted at full thrust. The roar of air about him became no more than a loud rushing, the rushing became a whisper so that he could hear again the complaining whistle of the jets. He had been falling at such a speed that full retro-thrust only saved him by a hundred feet from hurtling through the transparent tepee and hitting one of the megaliths. He bounced up again like a cork, remembering Juno.

57

They rendezvoused at three thousand feet, two dull green glowworms who recognized each other in a way that neither could understand.

Dion stabalized. Juno jetted close.

"Psycho!" she sobbed. "Deadhead! Fool!"

"Medieval fool," he conceded. "The joke is on both of us. They call it life."

"Oh Dion, you hazy crazy word juggler! Why did you do it? I nearly died for you."

He laughed. "I nearly died for myself. . . . It's a very cold champagne that God serves on the ceiling, shrivel-womb. You should try it some time. There comes an interesting moment when the stars go dark."

"I'll never jet with you again."

Dion was enjoying himself. "You will. Where I lead, you'll do your tiny dom-best to follow. And each time you fail, you will get a little nearer to understanding the difference between men and women. Message ends."

Juno was silent for a moment or two. Then she said, "Let's touch down at Reception. They must have radar-tracked you. They'll wonder what kind of oddball bounces against the sky."

"Let them wonder," he retorted equably. "And if anyone should ask, say: 'Dion Quern, master of nothing, has briefly surveyed his kingdom . . .' Have you ever tasted your own frozen blood?"

"My dear one," said Juno helplessly. "Sometimes, I even think I understand."

Dion looked below him, at the hectic, illuminated circle around Stonehenge and then at the sea of darkness that covered the featureless plain.

"Reception can wait," he said. "There will be time enough to entertain Victoria of England with the social inanities of our age. But for five minutes, wench, you can lie with your legs open behind a thorn hedge like any honest slut would have done in the last two millennia. Then you too can taste the taste of frozen blood."

Juno, glancing toward Stonehenge, saw the royal stand-

58

ard break in a spotlight glare. She opened her mouth, but no sound came. Dom and harlot, Dion was pleased to note, were at war with each other. The victory was a foregone conclusion.

Silently, almost submissively, Juno jetted down into the darkness.

FOURTEEN

The Halloween party that had threatened to hit an all-time nadir in the international social limbo had, in fact, turned out to be quite memorable. Victoria the Second delicately adjusted the bandage on her head as she sipped her iced Polish white spirit and surveyed the general wreckage with some satisfaction.

Great flaps of metal foil, torn from the megaliths, rustled complainingly in the light breeze. Strips of transpex drifted through the air like half-materialized ghosts. A couple of dead white cocks glared malevolently at each other on the now frosty ground. And somewhere in the outer darkness a few traumatized sports and wounded Peace Officers were drinking and singing themselves into oblivion. The Russian ambassador had retreated into hysterics, the European Pro-consul had been carried off and doubtless raped by the pirates, the Prime Minister had a broken arm and a laser burn on her breast, and Victoria herself had been hit by a falling broomstick . . . Yes, it had been a memorable occasion.

Victoria had not yet received the casualty list, but there could hardly have been more than a dozen absolute deaths and perhaps four or five temporary deaths. The surgeons were already at work in the resuscitation unit; so it should not be long before a few lucky Peace Officers and less lucky pirates received the resurrection and the life.

At one stage it had seemed a cast-titanium certainty that the party would never jet. The professional witches hired for the occasion had produced nothing more shattering than the ritual defloration of an infra virgin by six Happyland-inspired warlock zombies, a group hypnosis that was less spectacular than the cabaret at the old Café Royal, the sacrifice of a goat and two cocks, and a ninety foot tri-di projection of Lucifer taking dreary liberties with an old-fashioned nun.

The beer was good. So were the black sausages, the ox blood cocktails, the corps de ballet, and the gladiators who had been bribed to fight to a temporary death. But somehow, the whole thing had begun to fade.

Until at midnight, when the programmed thunder and lightning had finished, the pirates came jetting down from the black sky with laser guns in their hands and sportive dreams of destruction in their retarded IQ's.

Victoria was delighted by the diversion. Left to her own devices, she would have knighted every single one of them. However, the conventions had to be observed—particularly when four of the intruders swooped on the European Proconsul, scooped her up in a large fishing net just as she was sampling the barbecued black cat, and zoomed up into the night sky again for a destination unknown.

It had been quite an amusing sight. The pirates had kept perfect formation; the net had been cast expertly; and before she realized what was happening, Josephine had found herself swinging crazily at five hundred feet, her life depending on the formation jetting of the four grade one aspirants who each held a corner of the net.

Since the abduction clearly came under the heading of diplomatic incidents, Victoria was reluctantly compelled to do something about it. In response to her signal, the sovereign's escort—which on this occasion happened to be a

60

squadron of Life Guards—got itself airborne and in hot pursuit.

But by that time the pirates had mounted the second phase of their attack. Their laser beams cut the high transparent tepee into a mad carnival of whipping strips of transpex. At least a couple of the pirates, caught in the contorting tentacles of plastic, were snatched out of the sky and dashed to destruction against the ancient columns of stone.

By that time even the Peace Corps had realized that this was not just another of Victoria's surprise diversions. One by one the Peace Officers who had come as guests sped to the Reception area, snatched their jet packs and duty accoutrements, and became airborne.

At first the attack on Victoria's Halloween party looked as if it might have been the impractical joke of a few itinerant sports. But if it was, it was well-organized. As more than fifty of them jetted down in disciplined formation, the joke seemed less than funny.

Juno was one of the first Peace Officers to get herself into the air. Dion watched her with irritating bewilderment. One impulse goaded him to follow her, to see that she came to no harm. Another impulse held him back, persuading him to let the dom stew in her own crisis. Besides, these boyos from the fourth dimension were hotting up what had been a very cold piece of social discomfort.

By the time he had disposed of the second impulse, Juno had already departed and there were other things to think about. Particularly when a surprisingly small Guards officer fell out of the sky and inconsiderately died almost at his very feet.

She had such a young face—probably she was no more than thirty-five or forty. With multiple fractures in legs, arms, and pelvis, she lay on the ground, a tiny extinguished glowworm.

Dion cradled her head in his arms. She was hurt in too many places to feel pain. But an intense weariness came over her childlike features.

She uttered only six words before she died.

61

"Love me," she said. "Love me! Love me!"

Then the body became slack and she was just another dead dom.

He picked her up, oblivious of the general pandemonium, and carried her out of the circle of light, away from the grotesque null-comedies that were being played around the megaliths of Stonehenge, to a quiet grassy hollow where there was nothing but frost and stars.

He laid her down very gently and straightened the shattered limbs. Then he sat there silently for a while, remembering the taste of frozen blood, thinking how easy it was to stifle the tin warm worm of life.

Presently, he kissed her already cold forehead and was guiltily pleased to find that he had bathed it in tears.

He didn't say anything. There was nothing to say. There was only the disquieting notion that, dom though she was, she never had been an enemy. She had been nothing more than a sad little machine.

But even machines are beautiful. And she had been a very beautiful machine.

He loved her. It was easy to love someone you had never known. Someone with whom you would never make love. Someone whom you could never hate, despise, or grow tired of. It was easy—and heartbreaking.

By the time he got back to the floodlit group of stones, the attack was over, the wounded and the temporarily dead were being treated, and the absolute dead had been removed. Victoria looked very regal—and pleased with herself—in the bandage that covered her broomstick bruise.

There was no sign of Juno. Dion inspected the party debris, then worked his way through the casualty treatment area and the resuscitation unit that had obviously jetted down only a short time before.

Still no sign of Juno.

Not that he was disturbed, of course. By this time, no doubt, like many other Peace Officers who were now jetting back in ones and twos, she had abandoned pursuit of the stragglers and was returning to Stonehenge.

On the other hand, she might have collected a laser burn for her trouble and homed on the nearest domdoc for a shot or two before returning to get a full fix. Not that he cared. . . . Much. . . .

Nevertheless, by the time another dozen Peace Officers had touched down, he found himself walking to Reception to collect his jet pack.

He had Reception put out a call for Juno while he was switching gas tanks. Then, when there was no response, he lifted. Looking for her would be about as easy as looking for a black beetle in the Channel Tunnel. But Stopes, it was better than fabricating zero.

Besides, the party was over. And all the remaining marionettes were drunk, dead, wounded, or very tired. Apart from the fracas, it hadn't been much of a party.

It hadn't even been much of anything at all, he reflected as he soared above the megaliths and switched his headlight on to full power. The best happenings had happened before the event. He remembered vividly his few frozen minutes on the ceiling when the stars danced and then went dark. He remembered also Juno's oddly submissive reactions afterwards.

He savored the recollections. Then he thrust forward at full power and swept away from Stonehenge, rising slowly in ever-increasing spirals. The night—what was left of it— was still crystal clear. The stars were now dancing a saraband.

FIFTEEN

Dion had lost all sense of time. He might have been in the air minutes, hours, or since the beginning of the world —if, in fact, there ever had been any world. If it had all not been some grotty fragment of a figment, some loose connection in the solitary nocturnal hysteria of a landlocked, airborne flying fish.

He tried to remember what he was supposed to be doing. Assuming always that there was something he was supposed to be doing. Which was a big assumption. . . .

He tried to send himself a message. Finally, he made it. He spoke very quietly and distinctly to his brain, and his brain patiently unscrambled the message, considered it for a while, then reluctantly relayed it to the eye muscles.

Dion looked at his wrist altimeter. It was a monumental achievement. The wrist altimeter said six thousand feet.

He was cold and he was short of air, and the combination, after his previous experience, was worse than drinking surgical spirit.

There was some further debate with his brain. The discussion was a shade metaphysical, but both parties were fairly reasonable. In the end they decided to issue a joint communiqué. It was directed to Dion's semifrozen hands.

They were rebellious. But eventually they acquiesed. Fingers closed stiffly on the jet control. Dion drifted obliquely and crazily down to seven hundred feet.

And recovered his wits.

It took time, but he recovered his wits. And while he was

recovering them he jetted gently along on a collision course with destiny.

God, or whatever blank-faced computer runs the fancy, fading program of the cosmos, must have displayed a great sense of humor and/or a total disregard for the laws of probability. Or maybe He/She/It was simply intrigued by Dion Quern.

At seven hundred feet the English countryside was an almost featureless sea of shadows. Except for one flickering point of light about a mile ahead. Dion gazed at it, fascinated.

There was nothing else to aim for, and he was automatically homing on the target. He reduced altitude to two hundred feet and let himself be carried sedately along at a speed no greater than that of a man walking.

He had time to think. He had time to think about how he disliked everything in this dom-dominated nonworld and how, most of all, he disliked Juno Locke. Which, of course, was why he was looking for her. And which, of course, was why he found her.

She was dancing naked around a bonfire; and the bonfire was consuming what was left of the European Proconsul, who in the finest tradition of English bloody-mindedness, had been burnt at the stake.

Both the dance and the cremation ceremony were being observed with some enthusiasm by a group of perhaps a dozen sports who, still wearing their dark sky suits, prompted Juno whenever she showed signs of weariness by a nonlethal volley of laser beams.

Dion was too high to see the burns on her body and too far away to hear the screams of pain. But he was now sober enough to imagine.

What to do? He had no weapons. There were too many sports—even assuming they were loaded with Happyland. There were far too many sports. And he had no weapons. Except himself.

At two hundred feet still, he circled wide and thought hard. But thinking was not much use. In fact, it was a definite liability. Meanwhile, the remains of Josephine burned, the remains of Juno danced, new blisters were raised on her body, and the hopheaded sports were risking embolisms with their pseudoecstasy.

Thinking was not much use. So Dion, with a brief apology to his brain, cut it out. He changed his stance. Without thinking.

He changed his stance from vertical to horizontal. He dropped altitude, kept his finger depressed on the acceleration stud, and came in toward the group of sports like a guided missle.

The air whistled past him. The sports, like a *tableau vivant,* loomed hypnotically ahead.

"*Olé!*" screamed Dion as he hurled toward them.

In the first pass, three went down, direct hits—and Juno continued to dance. He caught a split-second image of her anguished face as he hurtled past the bonfire and out into the dark.

Then he swung in a tight semicircle and came back. The sports were ready for him this time. He collected laser burns in too many different places. But he didn't care. He already had nasty impact bruises on his head and shoulders. Laser burns were merely light relief.

"*Olé!*" Another four went down. This time his left arm flapped loosely, and he knew that it was broken.

The right hand still manipulated the jet controls. Past the bonfire once more, he swung again.

By this time the sports had spread out a little. They looked vaguely like a firing squad that he had seen in an antique movie. Three of the remaining four had laser pistols, but the fourth had something considerably older and —on this occasion—considerably more effective.

It was a vintage army revolver, caliber .45. As Dion hurtled in, the laser beams burned part of his sky suit to liquid rubber, but the second bullet from the revolver—to the amazement of all present—passed straight through his heart.

Dion's dead body knocked out one more sport before it crashed heavily to earth.

The survivors, when they had pulled themselves together, looked up at the sky, expecting further intruders.

They were not disappointed. The headlight beams of Peace Officers making a systematic sweep swung distantly through the October night like wands of pale fire.

After hurried consultation, the remaining sports decided to jet. The night's work had qualified them all for grade ones. But they were in no hurry to collect. They ran for their jet packs and lifted discreetly away from the bonfire.

Josephine's charred body sank listlessly into the embers.

Under the influence of deep narcosis, and reflexes conditioned by laser beams, Juno continued to dance.

Somewhere an owl hooted. And the world was curiously still.

PART TWO

THE TEN THOUSANDTH DOOR
I know Death hath ten thousand several doors
For men to take their exits.

—John Webster

ONE

On the sixth day of resurrection, Dion Quern had a visitor. On the third, fourth, and fifth days of resurrection he had also had visitors. But they were all the same, and they were all called Juno Locke.

This one was different. It wasn't lovesick, it wasn't full of gratitude, it wasn't female, and it was called Leander Smith.

"Greetings," said Leander. "He who was dead is now living. Unto them that hath shall be given."

Dion pressed a button and the bed raised him to semi-recline. "How the Stopes did you know where I was?"

"Dear fellow, you are too modest by far. Half England knows you are in the London Clinic. And the other half is still quasi-enthralled by your totally out-of-character derring-do. It is rumored even that the Queen proposes to knight you. Sir Dion Quern. Superb! What an aura of respectability the very words conjure. I must congratulate you. No one in the Lost Legion has yet achieved such notoriety."

"I am no longer in the Lost Legion. I contracted out. If Halloween was anything to go by, you're just a bunch of hophappy sados."

"Halloween was nothing to go by, Dion, friend of my youth. Also it was not even our party. For once—just for

71

once—a bunch of bored sports shot themselves full of bravery out of needles. Now they are doubtless scattered and shaking with fear all over this demi-paradise. . . . It matters not. What matters to you is that I have your life in my own tremulous hands. So reorientate by all means—but carefully."

"I have already reorientated, joker," said Dion without much conviction. "I propose to become a useless and extravagant member of this great society. The doms owe me a living."

"To say nothing of a rather dazy-crazy dying."

"That wasn't the doms. That was persons allegedly male, unknown—or maybe less unknown than formerly." He treated Leander to a sardonic gaze.

"Playback," retorted Leander calmly. "The Lost Legion was elsewhere, as I recall. . . . But whatever, Dion, dear friend, it matters not. You missed the message. I have your life in my hands."

"Words are just words. Make them say something."

"Certainly. You belong to me—or, more improperly, to the Lost Legion. If I say live, you live. If I say die, you die. Elegantly simple. Sad also. And, incidentally, quite expensive."

"Make it simple," snapped Dion irritably. "Tell it briefly and depart. I have quite a busy morning doing nothing."

"So be it. By mere whim—although my whims are never mere—I can execute you. Any time, any place. Let us pray that I never become absentminded, or homicidally drunk."

"How?"

"Ah, an excellent question. Observe." Leander took a small box about the size of an eighteenth-century snuff box from his reticule. He held it up for Dion to see. There was a tiny red button in its center.

"Be not skeptical," went on Leander. "This toy—miniaturized, transistorized, and for all I know, circumcised—contains for you the secret of eternity. All I have to do is press the red button and your tense is past. If I keep it pressed for ten seconds, you die permanently. If I lift my

72

finger before the ten seconds are up, you live again. What could be more simple?"

Dion gazed at the box curiously. Then he looked at Leander. The hopheaded coot was smiling. Big joke.

"Prove it," said Dion.

"Certainly. Have you any infamous last words?"

"Yes. Take a fast jet to Hades, find a snowball, and insert."

Leander laughed. "A squire of some spirit! But could one have expected less? Be of good cheer, dear prince. Styx and verbal stones are unlikely to break anything permanently. Meanwhile, may angels sing thee to a five-second rest."

He pressed the button, and Dion fell back dead.

Leander counted up to five carefully, then lifted his finger. Dion shuddered, took a deep breath, and came back to life.

He rolled his eyes for a moment or two, licked his lips, and sat up once more. "God rot you! What kind of jack lurks in that little box of tricks?"

"No jack. Simply the ace of spades. I trust you slept well?"

Dion, considerably shaken, retreated into nonchalance. "That's the second time I've died this week. It is getting monotonous."

"The monotony could, of course, be permanent," warned Leander lightly. "One hopes, naturally, that permanence will be somewhat delayed."

"How the Stopes did you do it? And why?"

"Patience, friend of my youth. One at a time, the how taking precedence over the wherefore. . . . You were shot through the heart, were you not?"

"So?"

"Therefore you now have an electromechanical heart. A micropile provides the energy, and the whole ensemble is presided over by an electronic timing mechanism. My snuff box merely overrides the timing mechanism. As I remarked, it was somewhat expensive. Surgeons cannot be blackmailed these days, only bribed. I hope you justify the cost. To say nothing of the risk. There are those who could have collected a grade one for this dark gambit."

Dion was at a loss for words.

"I see you are at a loss for words," went on Leander. "No matter. They will come, I'm sure. Meanwhile you really should register the fact that in the midst of life there is a small red button. Once you have accepted this, you will doubtless enjoy a long and fruitful coexistence."

Dion, meanwhile, had found some words. Three of them. "Now the wherefores," he demanded tensely.

"Public relations plus pragmatism," explained Leander. "You are now a character of some status, *mon ami*. By virtue of the fact that your built-in death wish compels you to make like a misguided missile when you see Peace Officers prancing naked through the dewy night while the European Proconsul is fried medium rare. So our hero faces fearful odds and virtue triumphs. It was anticipated that the doms would fete you—which they will, given point five of a chance. So, inevitably, the Lost Legion decided to fete you. Nothing personal, you understand. But a boyo who has the entry, for example, to New Buck House is precious beyond synthetic rubies when it comes—and it will—to blowing a few big doms to glory. . . . So there was merely the question of ensuring your loyalty—which, if I may say so, has been accomplished in the most sensible if extravagant way. And how do you like that?"

"I don't. What do you want me to do?"

Leander smiled. "My! What eagerness! What impatience! Nothing at all, dear lad. At least, not yet. The time will come—quite quickly now, I imagine, for life is full of interesting little surprises. But meanwhile, rest, stay tranquil, and meditate. Also do not forget the small red button."

"Do me a service," said Dion bitterly. "Drop from a great altitude."

"That would only embarrass you." Leander turned toward the door. "Relax, Dion. Also get well soon. Incidentally, don't try to switch to a new tin heart. The one you

74

have is the best available. Furthermore, anticipating such temptation, it is triggered to go boom if anyone tries to switch it. So let's keep our lovely secret. *Salaam.*"

"Get scrofula," advised Dion without much hope.

TWO

"Milk or lemon?" inquired Victoria. She was pouring from the same teapot that had been used domestically by the Great Queen at Balmoral some two centuries before.

"Milk, please," said Dion.

"Sugar?"

"Two lumps."

"Dear boy," said Victoria, handing him the cup. "You have such a pleasant manner, and matching profile. Your little Peace Officer must feel frightfully lucky. . . . What about a KCEP?"

"Playback?"

"Sorry, love. But the intimate social occasion has to be polluted slightly by sordid matters of business. I have to do something about you. The vids have been squawking like mad. So if it is not too wearisome, I thought of making you a Knight Commander of the Order of Emmeline Pankhurst. That and a bounty of, say, then thousand lions, of course."

Dion grinned. "The one will help me to bear the other."

Victoria smiled graciously. "I see our two hearts are beating as one. By the way, how is your new heart? I hope it's a good one. I gave orders for the Clinic to charge it to Disbursements B."

"It literally goes like a bomb," said Dion dryly. "I could

go upstairs three at a time—that is, if there were any stairs left that one would want to go up three at a time."

"I'm so glad," said Victoria with a smile. "So terribly, terribly glad. Of course, if you could have saved poor Josephine, I might have been able to give you a duchy. Still, one can't have everything. They tell me she didn't suffer too much. The poor child was already clear of the ground before those dreadful peasant fellows lifted her. Even so, her departure has created a delicate diplomatic situation. Understandably, the Federation is not wildly enthusiastic about sending us another Proconsul. . . . What did you think of the party?"

"Dead," said Dion.

"Oh. You didn't care for it?"

"It had its moments."

"I thought," said Victoria carefully, "that it warmed up somewhat toward the end. . . . You will, of course, stay here at Buck House for the night?"

"I have a notion Juno will be waiting for me at London Seven. In fact, I expected her to collect me at the Clinic."

"She was required not to," explained Victoria. "Reasons of State. So you'll stay the night. That's already programmed. In view of the fact that your little dom was mildly abused in the course of her duty, she is being awarded a year's sabbatical. Full emolument and all that twaddle."

"You are very kind."

Victoria laughed. *"Noblesse oblige. . . .* Which works two ways, Sir Dion Quern. There will be lots of fearful creatures at dinner, I'm afraid. But I think I'll see you later. Yes, I'm sure I'll see you later. Now go and have a bath, sweet child. And smother yourself in oil. There's nothing so delights my royal taste as a gleaming silky skin."

THREE

After dinner Dion found himself cornered by the Prime Minister, the leader of Her Majesty's loyal opposition, a submarine farmer who had recently been honored for her intensive breeding of whales, and the British winner of the decathlon in the last Olympic Games.

The four doms had him more or less to themselves while Victoria circulated around her salon in the course of queenly duty. There were not many males present, he noted. In fact, a rapid count told him that they were outnumbered by nearly four to one. So the four doms who held him in conversation were merely hanging on to their ration.

"Your motivation," said the Prime Minister, "intrigues not a little. I took the trouble, Sir Dion, to find out that you have already acquired three threes. This means—or ought to mean—that you are inherently antisocial. A natural candidate for a two, in fact. And yet there you go, performing quixotry in the stilly night. The inconsistency disturbs me."

Dom Ulaline Shores, Prime Minister of the United Kingdom, was a still handsome woman of one hundred and three. She had been born in the year 1968, in a world still dominated by men. Despite her reputed shrewdness as a politician, there was still some clinging remnant of the grace of a man's woman about her, thought Dion as he sipped his brandy. And there seemed to be a great sadness deep in her eyes. Maliciously, he hoped she had seen too much. Clearly, time shots would give her another half-century—if the spirit was willing. But since the flesh was too damn strong, quite probably the spirit would be stupidly weak.

"Inconsistency," said Dion, picking up the conversational thread, "is all that sorry little bedwarmers like me have left with which to confound our masterly mistresses. You will forgive us if we exploit it."

Two hundred pounds of muscle and bone vibrated as the decathlon winner laughed. "Bravely spoken, manikin. But there are those who would be inspired by such sentiments to snap you in two."

"Meaning, of course, yourself," retorted Dion waspishly. "The point about the dinosaur is that it had obsolescence built in along with size."

"You are trying to tell us something?" inquired the leader of the opposition. She was about sixty, slender, monotonously beautiful, and flint-hard.

Dion had already drunk quite a lot of brandy—the doms freshening his crystal whenever its contents were reduced to a finger—and he was also tired. Mechanical hearts with built-in detonators *might* be excellent for the circulatory system, but they did little to reduce mental fatigue. He wondered where Leander was at that point in time. It would be somewhat amusing to go boom at the palace, perhaps taking the P.M. and suchlike with him.

"Yes, I am trying to tell you something," he said thickly. "I am trying to tell you that you have played a bad biological joke, that you have sold the human birthright for a mess of contraception, that you have frustrated your own big breasts, that you have scrambled the eggs of creation. In short, that you have pulled the plug out of history." He hiccuped.

The doms all laughed.

"Wonderful stuff," said the Prime Minister. "You ought to be in the House."

"How many men—if any—are in the House?" demanded Dion.

"Eleven—I think. . . . They still have a certain odd sense of humor in the north and the northwest."

"Then it's a House of Ill Repute," said Dion vaguely. "It has eliminated imagination, creativity, and foresight from government. It's a House of Demented Dolls."

"Sweeping charges," said Dom Ulaline in a deceptively silky voice. "What evidence have you?"

"The sky."

"Elucidate, child."

"All the world's a cage," explained Dion, "and all the men and women merely bit players . . . What happened to the settlement on the moon, the laboratory on Mars? Where are the manned space stations and the starships and the jolly jokers who only wanted to freeze for a few decades while they drifted out toward the constellations? You killed them—you and all the other beautifully hygienic social machines. You took the mainspring out of man."

"Pardon the absence of a standing ovation," snapped the Prime Minister, "and keep your synapses operating, little one. There are things you should know. I was born into a world where space flight was the greatest thing since salted peanuts. When I was a child, the Americans had an orbital station and an expedition mounted for Mars. The Russians had a lunar laboratory. And two thousand million people here on earth were starving. There were enough hydrogen bombs to kill the human race seventeen times and enough left over to blast the Andes into the Pacific and turn Antarctica into a luminous desert. But infant mortality in India was thirty per cent, and China was carrying out five million abortions a year. And since the beginning of the twentieth century, people had been blowing each other to an increasingly mechanized glory. It was a man's world, little one. A man's world in which everybody was rapidly running out of time."

"What is it now?" said Dion savagely. "A worn-out, microminiaturized limbo where nobody starves too much, where nobody gets hydro-bombed, and where the psychiatric squads pick up the debris of original thought. A world where three quarters of the women are as sterile as robots and the rest are automated baby factories. A world where —if you are not an infra, not a sport or a squire—you can live till one fifty and buy yourself an orgasm a day to keep the domdoc away. Of such, dear doms, is the kingdom of decadence."

"Ah, a genuine messiah!" cried the leader of the opposition with evident delight. "He should be preserved in the Natural History Museum."

"I am preserved," retorted Dion, "in the Unnatural History Museum. It's all actually happening." The decathlon winner replenished his crystal once more, and he took a deep swig. "Let us have an auction, sweet doms. I am a marketable commodity. Who, wishing to test the metal of a messiah, will start the bidding at one hundred lions?"

"Two hundred," said the submarine farmer, a dark-skinned brunette, speaking for the first time. "Whales I am familiar with, but an eloquent porpoise might be fun."

"The joke is sour," said Dom Ulaline severely.

The leader of the opposition smiled. "Three hundred says it is still amusing."

"Three fifty," said the winner of the decathlon. "The material seems slight, but the spirit is interesting."

"How quaint," said Victoria, who had advanced upon the group unseen. "How fearfully quaint. I am afraid, dearest ones, that my bid consists only of the royal prerogative."

FOUR

St. James's Park was filled with all the lonely, foggy magic of a November morning. Dion stood patiently by the edge of the water with a couple of croissants he had stolen from New Buck House. He was hoping to feed the ducks. There weren't any. Maybe they had all emigrated to some far patch of Elysian mud where worms wriggled sempiternally in an orgy of self-sacrifice. Or maybe the poor disconcerted ducks had all been volunteered into the Lost Legion and were even now being fitted with explosive gullets so that when the doms fed them there would be some corner of St. James's that would be forever Aylesbury.

Dion was sad and confused. He was angry and undecided. And was trying to convince himself that he hated everything in the world except the wispy fog that London wore like an ancient negligée.

He was a walking bomb. A dead man who wouldn't lie down. A marionette at the end of an electronic string. A man who wanted to destroy the world of superwomen without getting his hands dirty . . . He was also Sir Dion Quern, a squire of some notoriety and independence—by grace of Her Gracious Majesty. And if all that wasn't enough, he had an aberrational compulsion to cherish an obscure Peace Officer whose two-dimensional mind represented the shortest distance in a point-to-point.

Above all, he was angry because he didn't know what he wanted. Also he was somewhat annoyed by the bitter knowledge that he was devoutly afraid of dying. Having tried it twice, he told himself dryly, it was high time he got out of the habit.

Which turned his mind to Leander Smith.

Who came in right on cue.

"How now, brown study," said Leander cheerily. "To brood in such a Nordic mist, a man must either be witless or an exceptionally bad poet."

Dion spun around and nearly fell into the water. "God rot you, bastard. Can't you leave me a solitary ration of *Angst*? And how in Stopes did you know where to find me?"

Leander smiled. "I forgot to tell you, lad. Our electronics twitchers had themselves a twenty-four-carat reciprocal-radar ball. Your tin heart is a telltale heart. We can follow your movements, find out wherever you are at any given nano-second. Very useful, in case you decide to hop to Ulan Bator. Then we simply press the button and mutter a few well chosen *sotto voce* words. . . . How did you enjoy your brief sojourn at Buck House?"

"Well enough, coprolite. Is your finger still button-oriented?"

"Not for the nonce, comrade. Others besides I carry the weighty burden of rebellion. Also—and this may afford some small solace—I am myself the bearer of a bomb in mine own aorta. The Lost Legion, brother zombie, plays for keeps."

Suddenly Dion leaped at him. Leander, taken by surprise, fell to the wet grass. Dion's fingers closed around his throat. He squeezed. He felt the divine power of destruction. He squeezed until the veins stood out on Leander's forehead, until his heels drummed noiselessly upon the grass. He squeezed—despite the clawings at his face, the knee in his groin—until Leander's face went blue and his tongue popped out in grotesque and obscene mimicry of a sexual endearment.

And then, half lying across his victim, avoiding the staring eyes, keeping his face averted as the life force ebbed, Dion noticed a single dewdrop on a leaf of clover. It was pure and round and beautiful. It was a glass cathedral. It was too beautiful to be so close to the sordid act of death by violence.

He relaxed his grip.

Leander sobbed, and whistled painfully, and sobbed again. Presently he sat up.

"Thank you," he croaked, "for services not completely rendered. Why, for two farthings, don't you save the rough stuff for the doms?"

"Because the doms didn't sentence me," said Dion, still looking at the dewdrop. "Because I had a war of my own to fight and you took it from me. Because I'm tired of people saying like it, or don't like it, or do something about it. And because, finally, I'm a stupid, contrasuggestible, hyperthyroid oaf."

Leander massaged his throat. "Message received. Now listen on all channels, stupid. The reason for this painful rendezvous I will transmit before you con yourself into further mayhem. At eleven forty-five precisely, seven days from now, you will toss an atomic grenade into the House of Commons."

"Alternatively?"

"Some joker presses both our buttons. The Lost Legion does not entirely dote on those who bet on the wrong horse."

"So pray for us both. Eternity, they say, is a great adventure."

"You're not going to do it?"

"I didn't say that."

"You're going to do it?"

"I didn't say that either."

Leander stood up. "Dion, what the Stopes are you?"

"I don't know."

"Then what do you want?"

"I don't know."

"For crysake, you have to know something."

"I know that I'm a man," said Dion. "I know that unless some psychotic clowns do something about it, I'm part of a dying breed. I know that the sun still rises and that the Dark Ages are upon us. I know that some bastard rigged it so that Dion Quern can take on Scylla or Charybdis . . . I know that I am cold."

"Let's go get some coffee," suggested Leander.

"On your way alone, carrion. I do not drink with procurers."

Dion watched as Leander disappeared into the thickening fog. Then he resumed his patient wait for the nonexistent ducks.

FIVE

After a time, he began walking. He didn't know where he was going or what he was going to do. Images rattled around in his head like a collection of ancient daguerreotypes. The box at London Seven . . . A big dom wearing hardly anything but a laser pistol . . . No Name . . . A sari and a fragment of verse . . .

He walked through the fog, not knowing where he was walking. Round in circles, perhaps. It didn't matter. Was there anywhere to go?

There was.

Suddenly Dion found himself at an almost deserted sky station near Parliament Square. Nobody but a fool or a moron would jet in such a fog. Which twice included Dion Quern.

The sky station attendant, a small, wizened sport who would clearly never make enough lions to collect his badly needed time shots, manipulated his mouth with some expressiveness. Dion did not hear the words. Waving aside the bee feature gesticulations, he thumb-signed for sky suit, audio-radar helmet, jet pack, and insurance. Then he inserted his credit key in the debit slot, collected his equipment, and put it on while the faded minion fluttered like a dying moth.

The audio-radar purred soothingly in his ears as he lifted. It screeched a brief warning note as he swung perilously near to Big Ben—the clock face breaking crazily out of the fog like the face of a frozen clown—then resumed its contented purring as he rose high over the river.

At seven hundred feet he broke clear of the fog and was enchanted by the brilliant sunlight. Below him was a carpet of gold-tinted cotton wool, stretching to the edge of the world. He looked down at it with immense affection—an aseptic veil drawn over the earthbound putrescence of mankind. Or womankind. Or both. It didn't matter, for the rot was dry and all-embracing. Abandon hope all ye who enter these vaginas. . . .

Enough of turning back the carpet, looking beneath the veil! Here was a lovely universe of nothing. Sun and blue sky and frozen dimensions of stillness.

He jetted east. East by the sun. East because it was as good a direction as any. He jetted east, hopping playfully from fog peak to fog peak, across miniature valleys and hypnotic contours, as if he were crossing some immeasurable sea on stepping stones that had been casually dropped by a nonexistent deity.

Time was abolished, turned inside out, stretched, shrunk, rolled into a ball, and torn into infinitely small pieces. He traveled east for twenty-one centuries, secure in the fiction that the journey would never end.

Curiosity was his downfall.

Curiosity was literally his downfall. He peeped through a hole in eternity, and suddenly needed to know where he was. He touched the jet control and sank gently into the carpet of cotton wool. The sun ran away in despair, the blue sky rolled itself up and tried to follow him, but it was smothered in the opaque gray limbo of the fog.

Down went Dion, slowly, gathering a frozen shroud of ice crystals as he sank.

The audio-radar stopped purring. Then it murmured anxiously. Finally it began to screech with a monotonous rhythm.

Regally, Dion ignored the warning.

A few seconds later, before he could actually comprehend what had happened, he was waist deep in the icy waters of the North Sea.

SIX

He stabilized.

It seemed the most idiotic thing to do. He could either have shot back upstairs into a gold morning or cut the jets and let the weight of the pack take him to the bottom of the deep black sea.

Instead of which he stabilized, enjoying a luxurious masochism as the icy water fought a winning battle with the heating circuit in his skysuit. His toes went dead first. Then the numbness crept less than stealthily up his legs.

He tried to think of Socrates and hemlock, and the sweet nobility of wrapping it all up in a final *non-sequitur*. Instead, he found himself totally absorbed by the slippery jet contours of the sea. There was a slight swell, and he was bobbing up and down gently like the float on a fishing line. He wished some goddam thing would bite or else the fisherman would make another cast. The jets whistled softly, a musical monotone. A permanent prelude in A flat.

The North Sea, wreathed in skeins of November fog, just didn't bloody care. Which was very satisfying. It was a totally disinterested party, and it didn't care one fragmented coprolite about the fate of Dion Quern.

The water swirled about him, sucking playfully without any conviction. And Dion bobbed up and down with the swell, waiting for a sign from that bastard fogbound sport on the black side of the sun.

None was vouchsafed. Fog there was at the beginning and fog there would be at the end. And between the beginning and the end there was nothing but indecision, vacuity, cowardice, dead legs, and about fifty fathoms of water.

"I am a dead man," said Dion aloud. He was disappointed because there was no echo and because nobody disagreed.

"I am a poet," he said belligerently. But nobody wanted him to prove it.

"I am an innocent bystander," he pleaded. But there was no corroboration.

"God blast it, I'm alone!" he sobbed. The North Sea did not dispute the point. The fog was no less indifferent.

"I'll pull out the plug," he threatened. Nobody admonished him.

"You'll be sorry," he screamed. But a gray sorrow already covered the bleak black sadness of the sea, and there were no tears left for Dion Quern.

So he cut the jets, sliding down into the water with a suddenness that totally unnerved him. There should have been a pause, or a hint of slow motion. Time for a last thought. But the speed with which the North Sea closed over his head was most disquieting. Even as he slipped into the depths he began to suspect a conspiracy. Also he did not much care for the salt water freeze-stinging his face.

Temporarily forgetful of certain obvious facts, he opened his mouth to utter further well-chosen words. The sea rushed in, and he panicked.

But he did not panic too much. Groping between living and dying with half-numbed fingers, he found the jet control and hit it to full vertical thrust.

Miraculously, he stopped falling to the bottom of the sea. Gas streamed angrily and noisily from the cylinders in his pack. He shot back up to the surface and out from the water like a demented porpoise heading for the stars. He had just enough presence of mind to switch to booster heat before he blacked out.

A limp porpoise, trailing vapor and drops of salt water, rose through the fog layer and plunged inertly up into the high gold world of sunlight. It would have continued up to the ten thousand ceiling where Dion would have undoubtedly hung until he froze as stiff as a Victorian paterfamilias, had not the pilot of a continental helibus possessed little faith in the wonders of automation.

She did not trust the tiny black box that was programmed to take the helibus infallibly to Brussels. So, instead of enjoying a brief narcosis as most pilots would have done, she sat on the control deck, grudgingly conceding navigational decisions and watching the foggy peaks flip by below.

In a moment of delicious unbelief, she saw Dion Quern arc swiftly toward the sun. She did not care greatly for what she saw, having had previous experience of off-lane sky walkers bent upon their own destruction. So she hit the M button, heaved to, and sent the second officer to life-bus station. As the unconscious Dion continued to rise tranquilly heavenward, the life-bus was launched to take up hot pursuit.

When Dion next awoke, he was in a bed at the London Clinic. Juno was sitting by his side. He had a terrible feeling of *déjà vu*.

"Nothing but exposure," said Juno cheerily. "You'll never know how lucky you are. Save your totally incredible explanation till we get home."

Dion gazed at her for a moment or two, collecting what —if anything—was left of his wits.

"Indecent exposure," he said at length. "I fully realize how unlucky I am, and I do not wish to go home."

Juno kissed him.

An hour later he was in the box at London Seven.

SEVEN

"I want a child," said Juno.

"So?"

"So you contracted to provide me with one."

They were sitting on the balcony bench, two hundred and fourteen floors up in London Seven, drinking coffee. Nearly half a mile below, the carpet of fog, which had remained tenaciously for two days, was now thinning a little. Dion watched the setting sun slowly transform it into a frozen crimson sea. The external atmosphere was cold, but the balcony was surrounded by a curtain of heated air streams. Thus was a bubble of summer preserved in the frosty altitudes of autumn. In the dying glow, the scene shimmered as light waves were deflected by the vapor content in a row of artificial thermals. The crimson carpet rippled and heaved as if it had suddenly decided to live.

"The prospect of artificial insemination is not one that fills me with total ecstasy," said Dion, collecting his thoughts.

"Reprogram. I did not suggest it. AI produces interesting statistics. There is a higher incidence of neurosis in both bearers and babies. I want this one provided the hard way."

"Hard for whom?" inquired Dion.

"Me, little troubadour. Do you think I *want* you to waste time and energy on an infra?"

"I might enjoy the experience."

"I shall be happy if you do. But the object of the exercise is to get a healthy child. Don't forget it."

89

"What has addled your transistors, shrivel-womb? Did that high-spirited little contretemps on Halloween give you an intimation of mortality? Are you getting old and sentimental in spite of time shots?"

Juno sighed. "Oh Dion! Why do you have to pretend that you are living inside a steel ball? You almost got yourself a permanent death for my sake. Is it so morbid that I should want your child?"

"Did they rape you?"

"Why do you ask?"

"Did they rape you?"

She smiled. "I suppose you could call it that. They shot me full of something and I groveled like a bitch in heat. . . . It doesn't matter now. The burns have healed, the psychodocs have processed me, and the only complexes I have are about you."

"Ha!" shouted Dion triumphantly. "You submitted. That's why you want a child. You submitted, and dear old Dom Nature resurrected the million-year programming. The lust-juice is irrelevant. You lay flat on your back, mind vacant as a lunar vacuum, while your body remembered what it was all about. You're trying to be an anachronism by proxy."

"Would it matter?" asked Juno. He was irritated to find that her voice and manner were entirely calm.

"Yes, flat-belly, it would."

"Why?"

"Because you can't cheat history forever."

"You're talking in riddles."

"That's nothing. I'm living in riddles."

"Is that why you tried to take a one-way ticket in the North Sea?"

"I was amusing myself," he snapped evasively. "I was playing follow-the-leader with seagulls and fishes. The kick rebounded, that's all."

"There's more to it, meistersinger. You were playing Russian roulette with yourself for a bullet." She looked at

90

him hard. "You've only been dead once. Are you already hooked on it?"

"We're all hooked on it, love. We spend a mere nine months getting born, so why take a couple of centuries for the dying? The great kick is to burn briefly and with some slight radiance."

Juno sighed. "That's why I want a child. I can still hear the ticking of the clock. . . . Something has happened to you, Dion."

"Yes. I saw a big bitch cooking in a bonfire and quite lost my head."

"No, something else. You were all right after you were resurrected at the Clinic. Something has happened since."

He grinned. "One knighthood and the royal prerogative."

"Still not what I mean. . . . Who was the sport who visited you while you were still horizontal?"

"Sleuthing becomes you. His name was Attila T. Hun and he came to see me about a tour of the Balkans."

Juno shrugged and was silent for a while. She sat gazing at the red sun as it slipped with an odd illusion of jerkiness over the western edge of the world. Then she began to shiver slightly, though the temperature remained constant at eighteen centigrade.

"You'll give me the child?" she asked at length.

"Why not? A new toy may divert you. You must be getting tired of itinerant poets."

"I love you," she said simply.

"Love is not enough."

"What is enough, then?"

"Absolute submission—and a world where men can breathe without having to ask permission from the nearest domdoc, where all women would be proud to see their bellies great with child. . . . You want a child, and you can have one. It will be a precooked, fresh-frozen, sterilized infant—and I wish you great joy of it. It will be a stranger to your breast and, if it's a son of mine, an enemy to your kind. It will have a love affair with your credit key and it will break a leg dancing at your funeral." He laughed

91

bleakly. "Yes, you can have a child. So you had better find me some poor, misguided, hungry infra whom I can ravish and cherish and age. Her wretched body will bear the fruit of my love for the price of a couple of time shots, and because of that I shall love her. Even if she's as dull as cabbage and as heavy as last year's potatoes, I shall love her. Because she will have an abject pride, an ugly beauty, and a fearful courage . . . And if you can understand that, you'll be halfway to knowing what's wrong with this orderly, hygienic limbo you ageless, faceless ones have created."

"I'm cold," said Juno, "and I'm tired. Let's go inside. . . . Do you hate me so much, Dion?"

"No," he said, getting up from the bench. "I don't hate you. But I'm damned if I'll ever weep for you. And that, dear beautiful playmate, is what really saddens me."

EIGHT

Dion was alone in the box, and the world was briefly and deliciously still. He had been alone for almost a day and a half. The luxury of it fascinated him. He began to feel that God—or whateversuch—was not necessarily on the side of the big chronometers.

For reasons best known to herself, Juno had flipped off on a lion kick. She had gone to Stockholm—so she said—to pick up some of the Swedish crystal that was too good for the Nordics to export. Then she was due to rendezvous with a chummy Interpeace dom for a beery evening in Munich. Then she proposed to surface jet to Rome for a few sex rags before high-jetting back to London on the morrow.

Allah be praised for the vagaries of alleged females. It meant at least, in this case, that one might have a little time to stand and steer.

Dion had plugged himself in to an antique movie on the vid. It was called *All Quiet on the Western Front*. He had found a mention of it in an old artpix catalogue and had requested playback from Centrovid. The computer had taken all of five minutes to fish it out of the National Film Archives.

And now, here was Dion, glued to the playback on a thirty-twenty wall screen. Some bastard dom had tried to reprocess the original as a tri-di color piece. But after five minutes of it, Dion had hit the request button and blown a few of Centrovid's microtransistors. So now he was on the original black and white, with its hazy halos, crackly dialogue, and motheaten dissolves. And he was enjoying every minute of it.

They don't make garbage like that any more, he thought sadly, helping himself to another German *altbier* from the carton of six that had been delivered via the vacuum hatch. And the reason was that doms were not carnage-oriented. They could not stomach the blood-and-guts motif that was the secret fantasy syndrome of all self-respecting sports and that had been the catharsis-trigger of all red-corpuscle-wearing males since time immemorial.

He watched the battle scenes, sad and searing though they were, with an intentness that verged on ecstasy. The images were horrible, grotesque, nightmarish; but they belonged to a vanished world of men. And because of that there was dignity in absurdity, beauty in horror, even peace in the terrible roar of ancient guns.

He watched with his eyes and felt with his body; but the tiny court jester who quipped around in his head still persisted in juggling with the problems of Dion Quern.

The tin heart under his ribs hammered loudly. Dion imagined—as he had already imagined many times—Leander's finger resting almost absently on the button. It was one thing to know that death is common to all. It was quite another thing to know that one's own death depended on someone else's caprice.

He gazed at the screen and took courage from what he saw. Men were dying untidily, crazily, and in vast quantities. They were dying of bayonet wounds, bombs, bullets, shells, fear, bad surgery, insane strategy, and sheer stress. So who the Stopes was he, Dion Quern, to complain about a bomb in his chest? Everybody carried a bomb of one kind or another. What the hell! There had to be an end to living.

And yet . . . And yet this was a different kettle of quandaries from when he had chosen to accept the possibility of death by sky-diving to the rescue of a naked Juno. That was a private luxury: this was just an infuriating bondage. And yet it was just the same kind of bondage as was being much appreciated by those poor inarticulate jokers in the antique movie. They were all living—and dying —with tin hearts. And for every one of them there was a Leander somewhere with a little red button.

Dion tossed the empty *altbier* bottle at the waste hole, which opened silently, silently swallowed, and closed silently. Then he reached for another bottle and flipped the cap.

He had toyed with the idea of telling Juno about the death box he was nursing at blood temperature. But would she have believed him? Yes, possibly. And if she had believed him, what would she have done?

Answer: She would have sent for the U.S. cavalry, smashed the Lost Legion, and uttered tearfully and with some emotive ejaculation while an obscure poet vaporized.

So that was a reasonable reason for keeping the merry knowledge to himself.

However, there were some small complications. Such as having to toss an atomic grenade into the House of Commons in—if Leander was a reliable informant—three more

94

days. Or such as not tossing the grenade and then simply waiting for the button-presser to press a button.

It really was quite tiresome.

And the most tiresome aspect was that Dion did not know what, if anything, he was going to do.

He wanted to smash the doms. But would that be accomplished by elevating six hundred loudmouths to a higher plane? And in any case, surely Don Quixote had a right to choose his own windmills?

"I think too ferkinmuch," said Dion aloud, still observing the sadly bloody drama on the screen.

"I feel too ferkinlittle," he added as an afterthought.

The bottle of *altbier* being emptied, he tossed it at the waste hole and selected another.

"Cogito ergo somesuch," he remarked definitively. A young German had just bayoneted a French officer and was praying to the corpse for forgiveness. The thirty-twenty was full of trauma and sadness and death.

He sank himself in the gore and proceeded to methodically finish the carton of *altbier*. Two-thirds through the movie and halfway through the last bottle, he was just contemplating the sublime possibility of calling up another carton when the plate buzzer made a nuisance of itself.

He listened to it for a while, fascinated, toying with the idea of changing the entire future history of mankind by simply not answering it. Curiosity got the better of him. He switched to receive and almost instantly the screen showed the face of Leander Smith. He was evidently in a public call box.

"Hi, savior," said Leander cheerily.

"Good night, bastard," retorted Dion, reaching for the cut stud. "You have a facility for being totally unloved and unwanted. I'm going through hell on the Western Front, and I require no assistance from anyone. How the Stopes do you always manage to plug in to my dried-up thought-stream?"

"Hold it," said Leander as he saw Dion move toward the stud. He held up the snuff box with his finger delicately poised over the button. "You wouldn't cut me dead, old sport, would you?"

"Yes, joker. If you were unable to cut me dead also."

Leander smiled. "*Esprit de corps.* I like it. There's not enough of it in the world these days. . . . You are alone, I trust?"

"Your trust is not unfounded. The good dom dallies briefly in Europe. Now state your sentiments and return to limbo."

"We have a rendezvous, brother ghost."

"I have not forgotten your foggy humor in the park."

"It is well. The assignment has been advanced one day."

"Give us this day our daily bread, and forgive us our trespasses . . . Who is playing games with what's left of my life?"

"The High Command, dear sibling. They move in somewhat mysterious ways."

"Their nonhappenings to perform," added Dion. "So I live less and laugh louder. Very interesting. Now let me return to my little fairy tale, and I will bid you a very good night."

"Not so fast, friend of my youth. There are details to arrange."

"So arrange them, and stop wasting the valuable twilight of my life."

"You know a bar, the *Vive le Sport*?"

"I know a bar, the *Vive le Sport*."

"I'll meet you there, midnight tomorrow."

"You may be exceedingly lucky."

Leander beamed. "I hope so. Otherwise, you may be exceedingly dead." He cut the connection, thus depriving Dion of the Parthian shot he had not had time to formulate.

Dion kicked the bed three times and wished Juno were present so that he could strangle her and drop her lifeless body over the balcony, half a mile to earth.

But Juno was not present, and there was no one to kill, maim, or make love to. Defeated, frustrated, he settled him-

96

self in front of the thirty-twenty and returned to *All Quiet on the Western Front.*

He was just in time to see the hand of a young and incredibly weary German soldier reach out to touch a butterfly. He was also in time to see an enemy sharp-shooter cancel the action with a bullet.

NINE

She was small, slender, and soft in the way that only infras could be soft. She was no more than a child—twenty-five, perhaps—but already poverty, or near poverty, had etched a few lines on her. Left to her own devices, she would age quite rapidly. By sixty—if she managed to avoid having too many children and lived that long—she would be quite old. Juno had found her singing for lions in a Munich *bierkeller.* She was mostly English, and her name was Sylphide.

Juno brought her back to the box while Dion was trying to scribble poetry with his antique pencil. He had been recalling his encounter with Leander in St. James's Park and was extrapolating upon it. He had also just crossed out the word dewdrop and substituted raindrop. One should not allow art, he felt, to get too perilously near life—particularly if the effect was maudlin.

So the verse read:

> *A raindrop grew into a glass cathedral*
> *and silence rolled like thunder in his head.*
> *He was asleep as one who is not living.*
> *He was awake as one who is not dead.*

97

Then Juno arrived with Sylphide, like a trireme with a sailing dinghy in tow.

"Hail, meistersinger. I missed you."

"Hail and farewell. I missed nothing. How were the sports in Munich?"

"More grateful than they are over here. What's that you're writing?"

"Your epitaph . . . Now, who is this child you have clearly stolen?"

"Her name is Sylphide, and she is going to bear me a son."

Dion inspected the girl whose womb he was required to fertilize. She was frightened and she seemed less than repulsive. He was pleased on both counts.

"*Enchanté de faire votre connaissance,*" he said with a courtly bow.

"*Merci, monsieur. J'éspere que notre connaissance sera très heureux pour tous.*"

"Your French is almost as limited as mine," said Dion. "How did this big bitch trick you into coming back to England?"

"Please," said Sylphide nervously. "Dom Juno has been very kind. She has already given me one thousand lions."

"Another thousand on conception," added Juno, "and then a thousand on delivery."

"Dead or alive?" inquired Dion maliciously.

Juno's good temper was rapidly evaporating. "Don't play too rough, little one," she advised. "And don't abuse my infra. She's paid to conceive, not to take punishment."

Dion began to laugh. "*My* infra! By the lord of misrule, what do you think you are—a seventeenth-century sultana?"

"Cut the transmission. We have spent half the day jetting, and we are rather tired. Now, talk nicely to the squawk box and get us something to eat."

At the mention of food, Dion realized that he himself was hungry. He had been drinking a lot, but he could not remember the last time he had eaten. He went to the vacuum hatch and spoke into the pick-up. "Accoutrements for three," he said. "First, avocado stuffed with shrimps. Second, pasta chuta. Third, Mexican strawberries with cognac. Fourth, Cheshire cheese, Danish butter, Finnish crispbread. To drink: two liters of rosé, half of Hennessey XO, black coffee, cream, demerara sugar. Ten from now. Out."

"Stopes!" exclaimed Juno with delight. "The man creates poetry in food also." Impulsively, she flung her arms round him.

"Unhand me, cow," snapped Dion. "The Last Supper was a dramatic occasion, was it not?"

"Signifying?"

"Signifying that life is frequently shorter than you think, and no one has yet calculated the square root of tomorrow."

Juno began to get angry again. "Who or what has scrambled your transistors, stripling? You are like a bear with a sore amplifier. If it's a fracas you are looking for, you can have it."

"Not in front of the child," advised Dion dryly. "Who knows what indelible impression it might leave upon her yet untarnished womb." He turned to Sylphide. "I presume that this will be your first?"

"Yes, it will."

"You wouldn't want to keep the infant?"

She looked at him helplessly. "What could I do with a child?"

"Ah, so. A fitting comment on our lovely world." He glanced at Juno. "Where does this innocent live, sleep, and endure the ravages of passion? Or have you not yet considered? This box is hardly big enough for a *ménage à trois*."

"I have considered," retorted Juno. "For the time being, Sylphide has a room of her own on the twenty-third floor. Later, we shall see."

"When the fruit, no doubt, is ripening on the tree," added Dion.

Further verbal skirmishes were cut short by the arrival of the meal.

While they ate, Dion learned a little more about Sylphide.

99

She was twenty-three and had been unclaimed. Her mother —still, possibly, alive somewhere—was a half-Dutch, half-English infra and her father an English squire. The dom who had paid for her conception did not live to collect on the investment, having got herself killed while carrying out research in synthetic viruses. So Sylphide had received the usual bounty of a State Orphanage until she was eighteen. Thereafter she had lived on domestic work for high-bracket doms, occasional prostitution with prosperous squires seeking refuge from their predatory partners and occasional work as a sponsong singer in bars, clubs, *bierkellers*, and brothels. She was already tired of life—which, possibly, was why she was prepared to settle down to a career of regular pregnancies.

"Don't you think there is something overripe in the state of Denmark?" inquired Dion when he had heard her story.

"I'm sorry. I don't understand."

"Nor does he," said Juno acidly. "I must warn you, Sylphide. Given three decimal places of chance, Dion will torment the life out of you. He's an atavism. It's his way of beating his chest. If he makes too much trouble, tell me and I'll reprocess him."

Dion ignored her. "I mean that the world is a dazy-crazy place when alleged females like Juno drip power and lions while you and your kind can only get by if you drip babies."

"But Dom Juno is a dom," protested Sylphide uncomprehendingly.

"Dom Juno is a dom," he mimicked. "What a lucid sentiment! A tree is a tree is a tree. And where the Stopes does that get us? They can't have programmed all rational thought out of you, child. Surely there is something left between your ears—or is it all concentrated between your legs?"

Sylphide burst into tears.

Juno picked up the bottle of Hennessey. "That's your ration, playboy. One more volley of antisocial rhetoric out of you, and I'll launch you down a long, long slipway."

100

Surprisingly, Dion was ashamed. "Sylphide," he said gently. "Dehydrate. Juno is right. Statistically, she's bound to be right once in a while, and this happens to be it. I'm a psych-happy, frustrated, full-volume midget, and I humbly beg your pardon. You have jetted a thousand miles to have your womb blown up, not to have your head opened. I am filled with chagrin, to say nothing of remorse."

Ignoring Sylphide, Juno looked at him anxiously. "Dion, what *is* wrong? Whatever it is, it's getting wronger and wronger."

"Nothing," he said lamely. "I'm the specter of a ghost, that's all. Forgive me, children, for I know not what I do."

He took the bottle of Hennessey from Juno and poured himself a substantial dose. He downed it irreverently in one, and then stood up.

"Midnight, monumental, looms," he announced enigmatically. "I must leave you briefly, dear playmates. I go to take counsel with one whose finger caresses most affectionately a tiny button. Doubtless in my brief absence, you will decide whose bed shall presently be glorified this night." He gave Juno a penetrating look. "In the interests only of futurity, I would recommend that the distinction fall to Sylphide."

TEN

The condemned man, thought Dion cheerily as he walked through the brisk November morning to collect an atomic grenade for the proposed elevation of the British legislature, had drunk a hearty breakfast. It being something of an occasion, he had allowed himself two prairie oysters and one bottle of champagne. In spite of which he still felt rather tired. What had been left of the previous night he had spent with Sylphide in her twenty-third floor box.

Since she was a complete stranger and an infra, he had made love to her several times and with considerable ardor. Enthusiasm did not have to be simulated, for she was, in a dark and oddly vacant way, very attractive. Also she knew exactly what to do with her legs, her arms, her breasts, and her tongue. Which was a considerable relief; for if one was going to dance, one should certainly not dance badly.

It was not, however, mere erotics that had kept Dion operating like a rabbit out to break its own record. Nor was it the result of a desperate need to please Juno. It was simply that whispers of mortality were scurrying about in his head like frightened mice. He thought it was very probable that he was going to die—by buttons or atomic blast or the laser beams of enraged Peace Officers. And while the prospect was not wholly horrifying or displeasing, it did have a disquieting touch of finality about it. Particularly since he had a notion that he had already used up his quota of resurrections.

In short, he, too—much to his amused amazement—desperately wanted a child. Posthumous, almost certainly. But what the Stopes!

It was a very sad thing to discover that one wanted a child. Particularly if one was about to high-jet Lethewards.

Sylphide had not been disturbed by his early departure. Literally, she had not been disturbed. Three or four energetic ravishments had been more than sufficient to remove all desire to remain conscious from her. She had fallen asleep almost at the point of final orgasm; and she had lain there without moving, her legs still wide apart, wearing nothing in the early light but the drowned look of a lost child.

During breakfast Dion had fancifully anointed her breasts with champagne and had said a few tender words over the smooth flesh that concealed a womb which might even then be making private arrangements for its future

102

expansion. But Sylphide did not feel the anointing and did not hear the benediction. Which, bearing all things in mind, was as it should be.

And now here was Dion, marching along to St. James's Park, a most un-Christian Soldier of the Lost Legion.

Leander had chosen the rendezvous for the handing over of the atomic egg with a fine sense of humor. It was the very spot where Dion had been distracted from killing him only a few days ago.

The briefing at the *Vive le Sport* had been nothing if not casual. It had taken place not in an oubliette or a chamber, but at the main bar, with No Name presiding vacantly and intermittently over the encounter like a worn-out basilisk. For reasons that he was unable to itemize, Dion had expected to meet a small contingent of the Lost Legion. He had also expected the hatching and conspiring to take place in some seclusion and with a surfeit of *sotto voce* precaution.

Instead of which there had been Leander only, and the projected atomic dissolution of Parliament had been discussed quite casually and openly over glasses of iced Polish white spirit. True, the *Vive le Sport* contained hardly anyone but No Name and two or three goose-cooked sports sufficiently withdrawn in flesh and spirit to exude nothing but vaporized alcohol and to receive nothing less than transmissions at one hundred decibels. Nevertheless, the great traditions of conspiracy were being needlessly flouted. It was, perhaps, too banal an environment in which to work out the details of one's suicide.

The plan, fully approved, according to Leander, by the High Command of the Lost Legion, was elegantly simple. As all great plans are. It merely depended on resolution, speed, good luck, and the flagrant idiocy of the person carrying it out.

At eleven forty-five precisely, one Dion Quern was scheduled to lay an atomic egg on the floor of the House. It would be triggered to dissolve Parliament exactly sixty-five seconds later—the time needed for him to vacate the cradle of democracy. Since such a delay was required for personal

103

reasons, he had, therefore, to follow the atomic egg with a freeze egg which, presumably, would prevent any MP who happened to be awake from rejecting the motion. The entire operation was to be carried out in a shroud of obscurity supplied by others of the Lost Legion who, according to Leander, would have already planted two mist-and-tear eggs in the Strangers' Gallery. These were programmed to release their opaque and noxious gases at exactly eleven forty-four and fifty seconds.

Thus Dion would rise briefly through a Nordic mist like some bright avenger from the distant shores of legend. Having hurled his bolt of divine destruction, he would then— weeping and coughing with the rest of the spectators in the gallery—make his way out and be lost in the stampede.

Leander would be waiting for him in Parliament Square with jet packs, and the two of them, from the lofty vantage of an altitude of one thousand feet above the Thames, would be able to watch Parliament blow its top.

That was the theory. It was quite a good theory. As such, thought Dion gloomily, it was destined not to work. Inevitably some damn thing was bound to go wrong, and none other than D. Quern, late squire and citizen of Greater London would be left sitting on top of the fireball.

He had, of course, been troubled by ethics—a fearsome ordeal even for a failed meistersinger. Was the tin heart of a frustrated poet worth forty metric tons of politically oriented doms? It was a nice question. But not one that was worth answering.

Perversely enough, decided Dion with bitter amusement, about the only thing that Leander Smith had done for him was to demonstrate beyond any shadow of doubt that he wished to live. To stay alive; to smell the late autumnal air; to feel pain; to feel pleasure; to get drunk; to write poetry; to listen to music; to beget a child. To beget a child . . .

It was an interesting demonstration—particularly since there was a high probability that it contained a built-in death sentence. . . .

Dion found that he was walking down the Mall—deserted even at this comparatively late hour of the day. It reminded him that London was, compared with the great hectic days of the late twentieth century, no more than a ghost town.

Its population had been halved, the festering sprawl of the suburbs had for the most part been returned to grassland, and the bulk of the populace either lived in Central London (quaint regency hovels, if you could afford them) or in the ten London Towers that rose phallically against the bewildered sky.

So the doms had accomplished something, he conceded grudgingly. They had smashed the anthill and had transformed it into a supercolossal funny farm. They had reduced populations, knocked out hunger, abolished the arms race, and taken dignity from man. Life—unless you were an infra pregnant for the tenth time, or an impotent sport with an ugly face, or a poet with a psychorecord—was a glorious and wholesome adventure.

So what the Stopes! And what better reasons for lifting a battalion of ancient female politicos beyond the reach of abstract nouns and time shots.

"Gentlemen in England now abed," said Dion to no one at all as he stepped into St. James's Park and made for the bridge, "shall think themselves accursed they were not here." He didn't entirely believe it, but it was a pleasing sentiment.

As he crossed the bridge, he noticed that the still surface of the water below supported a veritable superabundance of ducks. This time, of course, he had nothing to feed them with. The time was always out of joint.

Leander was already waiting.

Leander was always already waiting.

It was a quite formidable talent.

"Well met by daylight," called Leander cheerily. "I trust you slept well?"

"Well enough, gravedigger," said Dion. "I've been raping the future."

"Then let us, dear lad, create a small quantity of history for the future to remember us by."

105

Dion looked up at the sky and sniffed the air apprecia-
tively. "It's a fine morning," he said.

Leander grinned. "A fine morning indeed. But, as some
prophet or other must surely have said, a fine morning
cannot guarantee a lack of darkness at noon."

ELEVEN

The Prime Minister was answering a question about the
proposed National Day of Wake to mark the passing of the
late European Proconsul. Dom Ulaline was in good voice,
but her oration, thought Dion, was hardly the stuff of which
history is made. The time was eleven forty-four.

The Strangers' Gallery was practically empty. So were
most of the opposition benches. What was the point of
coming along in the flesh when you could flop in your own
box and, if you were so masochistically minded, take all
the political yapcrap you could stand by looking onto the
vid?

Most of the people in the Strangers' Gallery were tour-
ists—itinerant, culture-hungry doms (with their occasional
squires) from Pittsburgh, Poona, or Peking. Little did they
know it, but they were about to receive the raconteur's
dream.

Eleven forty-four and thirty seconds. Another twenty
seconds and this dom-dominated democracy would be en-
riched by a small quantity of mass-decontamination. No
doubt there would be transient sadness in the shires, but
loudmouths there were aplenty. And it would not be long
before some other P.M. was answering a question about

106

the proposed National Day of Wake for the hot curtailment of the present session.

Dion thought of Sylphide and fingered the atomic egg secretly and nervously. It weighed a million metric tons, and it was burning his fingers to the bone.

If he had been a praying man, he would have prayed that she had conceived. I am nothing but a pot-carrier, he thought hazily. I am a peripatetic vessel containing germ plasm, and my only worthwhile function is to fertilize every fertilizable female so that the earth shall inherit an untold quantity of Mark II Dion Querns, world without end. What the Stopes am I doing here, he thought. I should be elsewhere, laying a thousand infras, proclaiming the joyful gospel of eternal orgasm, filling an infinity of bellies with the greatness of child.

Eleven forty-four and forty seconds.

A fly alighted on the tip of his nose, and he sneezed.

The Prime Minister paused. A dom from Pakistan casually gave herself a block injection. A squire yawned. The leader of the opposition breathed deeply and discovered an interesting pain in her left breast. Dion shivered. And the sun broke through the clouds, sending shafts of light through ancient windows.

Eleven forty-four and fifty seconds.

The mist-and-tear eggs popped.

Balloons of opaque vapor expanded through the Gallery. The sunlight was canceled. Dion Quern became a fully automated marionette.

As the stampede got under way, Dion stood up and hurled his egg. There was something else he had to do, he realized drunkenly, with tears streaming down his face as the gas swirled about him.

Ah so! The freeze egg. He groped for it, being unable to keep his eyes open. Then he flung it wildly, having lost all sense of direction. And after that, he joined the general exodus, stepping heavily on the dom from Pakistan. She was thoroughly amazed to find that her favorite block had on this occasion produced a cry-fog through which English

107

peasants insisted on trampling upon her without, if you please, any sexual connotation.

Somehow Dion made it out into the sunlight. Goddammit, nobody stopped him. Goddammit, where the Stopes were all the Peace Officers? Goddammit, why wasn't he dead and why wasn't the House in orbit? Goddammit, why was Leander laughing so much he couldn't even put on the jet packs?

And why, for crysake, had somebody pulled the plug out of time?

The nightmare thickened.

Presently, with Leander close at his side, still laughing, Dion rose up over the doomed House, high over the Thames, waiting for the crack of doom.

It never came. Leander couldn't stop laughing. Even at a thousand feet he couldn't stop laughing. His laughter seemed to roll thunderously across the sky.

And the sun continued to shine quite calmly, as if it were just another day.

TWELVE

It was, indeed, just another day. The sun may have lacked warmth, but not determination. Its richly chilled light pierced the misty azure of the kind of sky that might once have delighted a character called Rupert Brooke. Dion, disposing luxuriously of Danish sausage and cider, sat on his Oxfordshire hillside gazing at nothing in particular and delighting in the retrospective trauma of a death that never occurred.

Diverted from an assumed collision course with eternity,

he was even too relaxed to murder Leander, who, likewise with sausage and cider, contemplated a kingdom from the past.

It was hardly worth breaking the windblown silence to discuss anything so mundane as atomic eggs that failed to hatch, but an obscure perversity compelled Dion to demand an explanation.

"What happened?" he asked lazily through a mouthful of sausage. "Did somebody piss on the fireworks?"

Leander, who had stopped laughing somewhere over Hertfordshire, gave him a benign and radiant smile. "Dear, dedicated scion of social justice," he murmured, "I love you quite truly."

"What happened?" repeated Dion. "Why no boom? Why no ascending radioactive blossom transporting its political burden to day-hidden stars?"

"Have you ever seen a purple dom?" inquired Leander tangentially.

"No. Have you?"

"No, my good friend." Leander belched and poured himself some more rough cider. "But we may yet be rewarded by that entrancing sight."

Dion sighed. "I fear I am about to be reprogrammed."

"Only by purest joy," said Leander. "Believe me. Only by purest joy. The atomic egg—as you have perceived with some brilliance—was no atomic egg. Death, at this stage, was not intended—it being only a dye bomb."

"So?"

"So, the dye is an excellent dye. It genuinely attacks the pigmentation of the epidermis. So all who sat in the House when you conferred upon them the royal shade will have purple faces etcetera for at least three months. Ridicule, dear lad, is a most terrible weapon. I fear there may be several temporary deaths by embolism before the government resigns."

Dion contemplated the pleasing prospect for several moments before it occurred to him that he had quite unnecessarily gone through hell.

"Why," he asked gently, "did someone not tell me—preferably, clown, yourself—that this was not an affair of mass domicide? Forgive the slight carp, but I might have slept easier."

"The High Command," shrugged Leander.

"Ah, yes, the High Command."

"The High Command, my hero, did not have quite the same opinion of your sterling caliber that I myself possessed. They wished to test you. Furthermore, they wished to test your resolution in such a way as would convince them that, when the time came, you would strike your true blow for the bent brotherhood without flinching. I have no doubt they are now satisfied."

Dion thought about it. "Speaking only for my selfish self," he remarked at length, "I am somewhat less than satisfied. Also, I think that at this stage I may resign from the Lost Legion with the loose equivalent of honor. I have done what was required. I accepted the hazard. The fact that the death egg turned out to be a dye egg is beside the point. I have no wish to strike any further blows. As far as I am concerned, the Lost Legion may eructate, ejaculate and—for all I care—bifurcate. The game does not interest me. *Consumatum est.* Now kindly press your button." He took a deep swig of cider.

Leander stared. Briefly, he was nonplussed. Briefly, Dion enjoyed it.

"I see you are nonplussed," he said. "What's the problem, matey? Did you forget to bring your snuff box?"

Leander so far forgot himself as to speak with a mouthful of Danish sausage. A small shower of protein accompanied his words. "You are no longer afraid of dying?" he inquired.

"Correction. I am permanently afraid of dying. I am possibly the most devout coward in the business. But most of all, fellow poltroon, I am afraid of not living. You and your Lost Legion are providing some slight interference with my plans for living. Therefore, let us settle the matter amicably by making me dead. Now where the hell is your

110

snuff box? At this point, death could be highly advantageous, since the cider is now finished."

"The contingency planning was at fault," apologized Leander. "I forgot to bring it. Who could have known that at the very apex of achievement—if you will permit such highflown verbiage—you would want out?"

"So much for the master planners of the Lost Legion," observed Dion contemptuously. "No doubt you expected me to weep tears of gratitude for mere survival . . . I've had enough, drybones. I know what your worst is, so kindly go back to base and do it."

"What about the future of mankind?"

"Compress it, stuff it, and extrude it."

"What about the delectable Juno?"

"Likewise."

"Ha," said Leander thoughtfully. "There has to be."

"There has to be what?"

"An Achilles' heel."

"Then find it."

"We will, dear necrophile, we will. You represent too high a capital investment to be canceled lightly. There are ways—there must be ways—of bringing you to heel."

Dion stretched and gazed benevolently at his companion. "I could kill you here and now. I could solve the problem for both of us."

Leander looked at him curiously. "Then why don't you?"

"For three quite stupid reasons."

"The first?"

"I am a fool."

"The second?"

"You are a fool."

"The third?"

"There is already a dearth of males." Dion stood up and reached for his jet pack. "After all, one should not make life too easy—or too difficult—for the doms. Thank you for the fun session. It was less elevating than was formerly supposed, but no doubt the aftermath will occasion a slight

111

tremor. . . . Don't call me. I'll call you. If I ever get so drunk or bored that I can't think of anything better."

He lifted from the hillside with a blast from the jets that rolled Leander head over heels.

At one hundred feet he stabilized, then turned east for an exhilarating hedgehop back to London. He wondered vaguely why he had begun to think of London as home.

Suddenly he remembered Sylphide. He wanted her. Not for love, not for sex, not for anything.

Except a child.

THIRTEEN

The government fell; the Purple Parliament remained in session; the Queen took to wearing a silver mask—thus making the gesture *de rigeur* for anyone who was anyone—to save the face of her ministers past and present; seventeen sports, eleven squires, five doms, and three infras all confessed to tossing the dye bomb; and life went on as before.

Dion himself had even thought of confessing. But the possibility that he might be taken seriously was an effective deterrent. It would clearly have brought him a grade two, which would have interfered not only with his occasional attempts to scribble poetry but also with the important discoveries he was making about human nature—chiefly his own.

Having left Leander—as he thought, for good—in the sausage-littered wilds of Oxfordshire, he had returned to London with as much celerity as the jet pack could supply. He was almost chagrined to discover that his absence had not been noted. Sylphide lay just as he had left her.

She yawned when he plugged into the vid to discover the score in the Mother of Parliaments.

She yawned when he told her of the sudden epidemic of purple politicians.

She yawned when he made love to her.

And she yawned when he again absently anointed her with what was left of the flat and now warm champagne.

She had not even missed him. Which was all just as it should be, he told himself with some satisfaction. She was a vessel—a much-ravished vessel of the future. And why the Stopes should a vessel of the future concern itself with matters that were not directly related to copulation, conception, and birth?

That she had conceived, there could be no possible doubt —if only because conception was fitting at such a time. When eventually this proved to be the case, he was not in the slightest surprised. In fact, he was convinced that he could actually recall the point of conception, when—at the second coming—secret battalions of living seed pulsed blindly like microminiaturized salmon toward the high dark pool of her waiting womb. There had been such a look on her face as if she—no longer Sylphide but a millennial woman with the secret of spring between her thighs—had known and shared the immense, silent knowledge of the moment of procreation. . . .

Now, with his hand on Sylphide's breast, his mind turned toward Juno. He was amazed to find that he could think of her with tremendous affection. She thought *she* was the one who had wanted a child; but in reality she was only the first one to realize that Dion himself wanted a child. Dom she might be, but her intuition had not yet been run into the ground by time shots. She had known. Yes, she had known. . . .

He got out of bed and, prompted both by malice and affection, took a fast pan up to the two hundred and fourteenth floor to see her. It was late afternoon, and she was not at home. Perhaps she had been mobilized out of her sabbatical to round up suspects for the morning's political mischief.

He waited for her, and fell asleep waiting. When she eventually got back, the black November night had surrounded London Seven in frosty stillness.

"How went the fertility rites?" she inquired coolly.

He grinned. "Well enough, madam. But that was in another country, and besides, the wench is pregnant."

"So soon? And how do you know?"

"The operation is not measured by time but by effort," explained Dion blandly. "And I know because I know. Also, an ovum sings when it is fertilized, and I have heard the sound of Musak."

Juno laughed and ruffled his hair. "What a nasty little troubadour you are. So you like her then?"

"She appeals to my sense of the absurd. What have you been doing with yourself?"

"Hunting egg layers—fruitlessly. And you—apart from the granted?"

"Painting politicians purple."

Juno looked at him severely. "Just the kind of pointless gambit that would appeal to a polysyllabic preshrunk Napoleon." Then she added lightly, "You can account for your movements, of course?"

"No. The only person who can is both pregnant and unconscious."

"All these allusions disturb me, little one. Are you in a mood to make love, or have you reached satiation?"

Oddly, he was in a mood to make love to Juno. He was in a mood to make love to her, he told himself, chiefly out of a sense of gratitude. She had given him Sylphide, and she had given him self-knowledge that he might otherwise never have gained.

But there was more to it than gratitude. And as he began to caress the firm body that seemed to have pride and power implanted in its every pore, he knew that there was more even than affection. Besides, he could take away her pride whenever he chose to, because he had already discovered

114

how to bring her to the very edge of submission, where pride and power were nothing and where that strong, beautiful body became little more than a contained mountain of unthinking, all-feeling liquid, effervescent with desire.

They made love quietly, expertly, taking their unhurried time to enjoy each other. Seeing the cloudy look in Juno's eyes, Dion realized dully that love was a two-edged sword. He realized also—perhaps for the first time—that though Juno personified all that he resented, she was, at the very least, a friend. He wanted to let the definition fix in his mind, without exploring it further. And because of that, he was genuinely amazed that friendship could beget such passion.

There was, of course, the inevitable comparison with Sylphide. Fancifully, he saw them both in terms of the eagle and the dove. But there was a time for all things. Even a time for eagles . . .

Despite rewards, threats, and a certain amount of what Victoria the Second called "discreetly ethical corruption" (a euphemism for the illegal use on a fairly grand scale of truth and disorientation drugs on half the sports of Greater London), the sick-psych who had delivered the dye bomb remained undiscovered. Autumn blended into winter, the days died coldly into each other, and the December kick of Saturnalia—with its attendant Father Green Shield—came and went.

Dion, undisturbed by any more baroque assignments for the Lost Legion, rejoiced in the continued absence of Lucifer (otherwise Leander Smith) and came to believe that since he had not dropped dead, his resignation must have been accepted in more or less good grace as a *fait accompli*. Or just possibly, perhaps, Leander or his minions were still needling some remote haystack in search of an Achilles' heel.

Whatever the answer, Dion Quern was too busy being quasi-human to take much time off for contemplative speculation. He passed his days eating, drinking, occasionally scribbling, and making merry, inordinately pleased by the confirmation of approaching paternity and wallowing nonchalantly in the quite different love of two quite different women.

And therein lay the Achilles' heel that an off-stage Leander waited patiently to discover.

FOURTEEN

Winter dissolved wetly into spring. Sylphide's belly and breasts became gently swollen. Dion had written a score of poems, one or two of which might just possibly survive him. And Juno had fallen out of her jet pack from a sufficient altitude to buy a country retreat.

The retreat was a disused nineteenth-century farmhouse, built solidly, bleakly, and enduringly of Derbyshire stone in the Vale of Edale. Edale, one of the more spectacular valleys of the Peak District, hardly knew that the twenty-first century existed. It was too far north and the terrain was too uneven for it to have been absorbed by the regional agricultural collectives. There was no point even in establishing hydroponics towers there, since these could be run far more efficiently and profitably near to the big cities.

So Edale, satisfactorily isolated from the twenty-first century, and almost deserted except for hill sheep and a few eccentric human refugees, was quite ideally situated for making love, giving birth to children, or scribbling verses. Another thing that recommended it from Dion's point of view was that it was two hours by jet pack from London. Even a helicar could not make it in less than forty minutes.

Juno still kept her box in London Seven. But Sylphide, being disgustingly happy in pregnancy and therefore something of an affront to any self-respecting dom, had been exiled to the farmhouse—appropriately named Wits' End by Dion. A little to Juno's surprise, and occasioning slight but continuous bruising to her ego, Dion chose to spend more time at Wits' End than at London Seven. Each time she herself went to visit Edale she felt vaguely like an intruder.

She had wanted to insulate the walls, build in pre-serve and disposal mechanisms, put in heat exchanges and tele-communications, and even reroof the house with a helideck. But Dion had blocked all these plans effectively. He had declared that if Wits' End was to be raped by technology, he would never come to it again.

So the stone walls and stone roof were retained, ice-cold water was pumped up from the bowels of the earth by an antique two-stroke, and log fires burned noisily on the ancient hearth. There had been an extensive search for period furnishings—brass bedsteads, old mattresses, a heavy black dining table, antique carpets, a couple of rocking chairs and a davenport, cut-glass oil lamps, even a gramo-phone and a picture of the Monarch of the Glen.

The final effect was claustrophobic in the extreme. Dion loved it, Sylphide tolerated it, and Juno loathed it. Juno loathed it because at Wits' End an era had been recreated where women were nothing but chattels. Dion loved it for the same reason. And Sylphide, apparently unaware of the pyschophilosophical implications, simply reveled in the windy silence of the valley, the frequency of Dion's con-tinued lovemakings and the subtle smugness of pregnancy.

The relationship among the three of them was exceed-ingly complicated, but workable. Juno wanted a child—specifically Dion's child—and she was prepared to tolerate much to acquire it amicably. Dion also wanted a child and wanted consciously to love the woman who bore it, want-ing to demonstrate that what he believed to be a natural relationship was the only one it was possible to fully enjoy. This did not prevent him from desiring Juno—or from needing her. There were times when he could happily have

117

broken a water barrel over Sylphide's head—her conversation being somewhat limited—and at such times Juno was the perfect antidote. But Juno was, by herself, not enough. Nor was Sylphide. Therein lay his quandary. He was looking for one woman whom he could wholly love, yet he could only find different aspects in two quite different women. As for Sylphide, she wanted little but security and physical fulfillment. Granted these, she was happy enough in her role of reproductive vegetable.

There were times—very frequently—when Juno tired of the Wits' End pattern of existence and had to go back to London and place her finger on the pulse of the city. There were times—infrequently—when Dion had to do the same. But they rarely went together.

It was on one of these rare occasions, when they were in the box at London Seven after an evening's slumming and alcoholic jollification in the West End, that Leander put a call through on the plate. The buzzer sounded, and Dion, being nearest to the receive stud, took the call.

As soon as the face showed on the screen Dion hit the cut stud. Leander's face dissolved almost in the instant that it had formed—but not before Dion had registered a triumphant gleam in the eyes that stared briefly and sardonically at him. He waited by the plate, motionless and numb for a few seconds, wondering if he was about to drop dead or if the call was about to be repeated. Nothing happened. Perhaps Leander simply was not in the mood for buttons.

Juno noticed his tenseness and had caught a fleeting glimpse of Leander. "Who was it, love?" she said lightly. "A specter from your terrible prehistory?"

"Combined, possibly, with an intimation of my terrible future," remarked Dion enigmatically, wiping his forehead. Then he pulled himself together. "No one you would know, flat-belly. He moves in the low and vicious circles from which you have abstracted me with kindness, constancy, and an embarrassment of lions."

"You swallow when you lie."

"I also swallow when I don't."

"Then come to bed and show me a sample of the merchandise you squander on Sylphide."

"Jealous, shrivel-womb?"

"No. Only impatient, stripling."

He leaped into bed with some alacrity. It was one way of avoiding abortive discussion. But even while he was engrossed in loveplay, he could not forget the look in Leander's eyes.

The following day he deserted Juno and jetted north again. In Edale, a small, bleak world enclosed by massive hills, he felt comparatively secure and relaxed. He arrived, drenched and with some drama, in the middle of a spring thunderstorm. He threw off his jet pack but was too impatient to deal with his sky suit. He simply unzipped the front and scooped Sylphide into his arms.

He wanted to fertilize her all over again. He wanted to breed a hundred sons and have them all come marching, male and mature, in ranks of four out of the same tiny yet immense womb. He wanted to love Sylphide because fulfillment was already there even before he began loving her. He wanted to have a written guarantee of immortality.

"What is it?" she asked at length. "You come dropping out of the sky like a sex-crazed imp."

"I am a sex-crazed imp."

Sylphide laughed and then sighed. "You are nothing but a man, Dion. And you must not make me love you too deeply because you are Dom Juno's squire. And when the baby comes, she will send me away, and that will be the end of it."

"Blast Dom Juno," he said savagely. "I'll kill her. I'll strangle her till her eyes pop out. Then I'll drop her body in the sea from a thousand feet. Then you shall give me a son a year until we both die of exhaustion."

"You love her," said Sylphide simply.

"I hate her."

"You love her, and perhaps you even love me. But most of all, you love yourself."

119

He laughed hysterically and threw her down. But before he could do anything more, he fainted.

FIFTEEN

Spring passed into summer. It was a long, golden summer with day after day that began in the clear amber of sunrise and rolled hotly but serenely through to the luminous crimson of sunset. Dion now spent most of his time among the billowy hills of the Peak District. He became a great one for climbing. Not for him the easy trip to the summit with a jet pack. He went up the hard way—armed with an apple, a wedge of cheese, French bread, a flask of water, and his pencil and scribbling pad.

He had cut down on drinking and had stepped up on writing. He was beginning for the first time in his life to feel reasonably happy. He knew that it was all going to end, and—with some strange insight—he knew that it was all going to end in disaster. But for the time being, there were rosebuds to be gathered; and he gathered them.

Also, he turned back the clock. In the hills, there was hardly any way of telling whether you were in the twenty-first century, the twentieth century, or for that matter, the fifteenth century. The color of grass had not changed perceptibly with the passage of time, sheep still wore the same vacuous expressions that they had worn since that terrible dom Elizabeth the First had begun the long process of subjugating the English male, and silence was still silence in anybody's century.

Dion lazed his days away scribbling verse, thinking—and doing nothing. In the evenings he would come down from the hills and create a make-believe world with Sylphide at Wits' End. He would pretend he was a nineteenth-century yeoman farmer, blessed with a fertile and submissive wife. He would talk with great conviction about their nonexistent farm and how life would be so much easier when he had a tall strong son to follow behind the plough. He found an old Bible and read aloud from it. He found some old records, scratchy and hissing, and played them on the antique gramophone. He developed a taste for musical comedy because it was so incongruously absurd, and in the early summer evenings Wits' End would resound to *The Mikado*, *The Merry Widow*, or *The Student Prince*.

When Juno came, the spell was broken. Then he would switch character and become the twenty-first century roisterer—a squire who could drink any dom under the table and dish out enough sex to excite the admiration of the Director of the Freudian Institute.

He knew instinctively that he was running out of time. He knew, even if Sylphide's now heavily swollen belly did not remind him, that the halcyon days were almost over. He knew that presently Dion Quern, prevaricator extraordinary, would have to decide whether to grow up or regress totally into a dreamworld.

At the beginning of August, Juno activated the trigger mechanism. Dion had wanted Sylphide to bear her child—as countless women in unnumbered generations had previously done—at home and unattended. Juno, on the other hand, wanted Sylphide to enjoy all the glorious and aseptic benefits of the London Clinic.

As Juno had taken the elementary precaution of committing Sylphide to proxy birth by contract, thus making Juno the legal owner of any issue, she could—if necessary —have enforced her decision to have her property delivered at a place of her own choosing.

It wasn't necessary. Sylphide was quite happy to go to the Clinic. Dion was the only one who seethed.

The baby was born in August. It was, as Dion had confidently expected, a son. There were no abnormalities, no aftereffects. The blood-mother, having been allowed the luxury of hypnobirth (at an extra five hundred lions) was hardly aware that delivery had taken place; and the infant, a fine red-faced eight-pounder, bawled as lustily as might be expected from a male child thrust precipitately into a world of women.

Eight hours after birth a touching family group was assembled. Sylphide, having had her first saline swim, lay propped up in bed looking conventionally radiant on two cc's of Happyland. Dion stood on her right, Juno sat on her left, and the infant grumbled drowsily in its air hammock at the foot of the bed.

"I shall call him Jubal," said Juno in a businesslike voice. "You will breastfeed for two weeks only, Sylphide; then he can go onto formula. I'll take possession at the end of the third month, but if you wish, you can be retained until he's ready for basic programming."

Sylphide beamed. "You are so good to me, Dom Juno." She had always called Juno Dom Juno. It was an attitude of subservience that made Dion wince.

He winced. He also stamped his foot. And raised his voice.

"God save us all!" he snapped, looking at Juno with eyes of hate. "So you intend to play the farce through, bitch?"

"The child is mine," said Juno calmly, "according to contract and payment. What have you to complain about, stripling? You've had your fun, and you have lived well. Spare us the tantrum. It's too exhausting."

"So is life," he retorted, "and love, and copulation. In fact, the only thing that isn't too tiring is death."

"Thus speaks the philosopher."

"Please, Dion," pleaded Sylphide. "Dom Juno knows best."

"Dom Juno knows best!" he shouted, glaring at her. "Has it dawned upon you, you big-breasted, emptyheaded infant-vending machine, that, but for the unthinking efforts of your kind, the doms would die out in a generation?"

122

Sylphide wanted to cry, but the Happyland kept her smiling brightly.

"That's enough, troubadour," said Juno. "Why don't you head for the nearest bar and gain some poetic inspiration?"

"Enough!" roared Dion. "By Stopes, enough is the dirtiest word in the English language." He took a deep breath and tried to match Juno's calmness. He failed. "I am asking you," he said icily, "to let Sylphide keep it. I am asking you because we have lain joyfully together, and because you have intelligence, and because this is something I want."

"There is something I want also," said Juno. "Your child . . . Our child."

He laughed. "*Our* child! I gave affection and lust and a brigade of alcoholic semen. Sylphide gave her body. What the Stopes did you give?"

"An unlimited time contract with a starving meistersinger, a birth contract with a regressing infra, and three thousand lions," retorted Juno. "And if you want to get maudlin, I also gave affection."

"If you keep the baby, I'll dissolve the contract."

"Dissolve it. A permanent son is a fair exchange for an itinerant troubadour. When he's old enough to develop a sense of humor, I may even tell him about you."

Dion leaped across the bed, his hands reaching for Juno's throat. She was too surprised to avoid him, and he connected. The beautiful body writhed as his fingers tightened; and he was only saved from destroying both Juno and himself by Sylphide breaking a water carafe over his head.

The carafe stunned him briefly and the cold water brought him back to his senses. His ear was cut and Juno's throat was badly bruised. He picked himself up and glared at her.

"I'm sorry, Dion," said Sylphide, still trying unsuccessfully to cry. "But you might have killed her, you know. You don't stop to think. Then there would only have been me left, and I can't keep a baby alone." She turned to Juno.

123

"He doesn't really want to kill you, Dom Juno. It's just that he gets excited. But of course, you know that."

They both ignored her.

"I'm asking you not to take the child from her."

"I heard you the first time. The child belongs to me."

"Then you will never see me again."

"So?"

"So you keep one, shrivel-womb. But I'll keep Sylphide, and there will be more."

"Your privilege, stripling." She smiled faintly. "If you care for that sort of thing."

"I'll also keep Wits' End. It pleases me."

"It pleases me also. And it happens to be my property."

Dion mopped his ear.

"Please," said Sylphide, managing at last to cry, "please don't alienate on my account."

"Silence, woman," said Dion, not looking at her. He faced Juno. "Then I'll pay you an appropriate price for Wits' End—the pile of trove some bastard dom gave me for saving your life."

Juno looked at him, white-faced. She too was near to tears. But there was too much pride in her, too much conditioning, for them to fall.

"Save your lions, sport," she said coldly. "The hovel is yours. You will need all the trove you can get if you are going to play the peasant."

"Better for me to play the peasant," he retorted, "than waste any more of my time pouring a stream of life between your barren legs."

Then, without even glancing at Sylphide, he went from the room.

SIXTEEN

Juno and Dion did not meet again in the flesh until shortly before the thin vein of poetry in his rebellious head was to be cauterized forever, and the lodestar of his imagination sent spinning dizzily until it drowned in a psychic maelstrom. Meanwhile, after Jubal (surnamed Locke) had been handed over to his legal owner—and to the new infra who would attend to his bodily requirements—Dion took Sylphide back to Wits' End, the quasi-pseudo-Victorian retreat in the hills that had become more satisfying to him than anything that he could find in the twenty-first century.

The long summer seared itself into a dry, bronze autumn. The leaves fell, and the scent of unimaginable journeys filled the air. Realizing, perhaps, that Time's winged chariot was not decelerating, he went into a brief final burst of creativity. Not poetry this time, but a series of letters. A series of letters to the true son he might never have but of whose future existence he did not entertain the slightest doubt. A series of letters about nothing and everything. About the pattern of dew on the grass; about the clouded look in a woman's eyes; about loneliness and about getting drunk; about all the things that a man had to do and be and know merely in order to remain a man. He wrote also about practical things—such as how to steal from doms without technically breaking the law and how to keep one's pride on an empty belly. The pencil was worn down to its last three inches; the antique writing pad was almost finished. And so was Dion Quern.

But he had just about enough time left to complete two important tasks. The first—and the easier—was that of getting Sylphide pregnant once more. The second—and one that was difficult beyond comprehension—lay simply in communicating to her what little he knew about love. Love as distinct from desire; love as distinct from gratitude or loyalty; love that was simply a by-product of the tremendously undetectable act of discovering.

Sylphide just did not understand about love. Or at least, she did not understand what Dion meant by it. For her it was a commodity. You could manufacture it, buy it, sell it, invest it. It was a practical thing of some functional value—and it could be mass-produced, tailor-made or even marketed as instant affection.

For Dion it was quite different. Sometimes it was an animal that rampaged inside his body, clawing at nerve ends. Sometimes it was a kind of loneliness that had to explode in passion. Sometimes it was a form of seeing, a way of knowing, a star-map marking the tortuous galactic route from one human being to another. Sometimes it was a nightmare and sometimes the blurred vision of an alcoholic. But, always, it was alive.

Lessons in love began in the bedroom, involving the common languages of touch and smell and taste. But eventually the syntax of emotion became too big for the bedroom, too complex to be expressed in erectile tissue. The teacher began to learn and the learner began to teach. And it was as if some joker had thrown a switch, reversing the stream of history until it ran back to the first man and the first woman.

Day merged into day. Nights were sometimes bright with ecstasy and frequently fogged with exhaustion. The October weather declared three weeks of Indian Summer, during which even Sylphide realized she was pregnant and even Dion realized that he had truly lived.

It was, Dion knew, all too good to last longer than a very brief lifetime. So he was not entirely surprised when, late in an afternoon of sunlit stillness, something that gave a

126

grotesquely poor imitation of a raven in the dying light came from the south, circled the valley once, and deposited its burden of bad news on the doorstep at Wits' End.

Leander cut the jets and stepped out of his sky suit with a radiant smile and a laser pistol in his hand. Dion noted the laser pistol and restrained his compulsively vacillatory impulse to destroy that which was clearly destined to destroy.

"What? No carillons of joy?" inquired Leander mildly. "Dear, rustic youth, it has been a long time since we elevated each other with wild aspirations to heroic manhood."

"Not long enough by a century, toad. How did you find me?"

"Surely you have not forgotten your telltale heart?"

"So all you had to do was lock on the beam. What kept you?"

"A small problem—the heel of Achilles. It was, of course, necessary to establish its location beyond a peradventure."

"And have you?"

Sylphide came out to join them. Leander smiled at her, almost absently swinging the laser pistol to point briefly at her stomach. "I think so, dear lad. I truly think so . . . I have been something of a voyeur in the past few months— purely in the interests of the Lost Legion, you understand. But the heel definitely exists, and therefore we are both in a position to negotiate."

"There is nothing to negotiate."

"You disappoint me."

"*À rivederci.*"

"A pity. I knew, of course, that you personally had expressed some slight disinterest in continued respiration, but" —again he glanced at Sylphide—"it did occur to me that your disinterest might not extend, as it is so succinctly put in some book or other, unto the third and fourth generation."

Dion sighed. "Negotiate is a word that has two sides to it, bastard. What, first of all, are you offering?"

"Complete and absolute Freedom. A full and honorable discharge from the Lost Legion."

"Dion, who is he?" asked Sylphide nervously. "What does he want?"

"What do you want?" said Dion.

"One small service to be performed on November the twelfth."

"Namely?"

"On November the twelfth," went on Leander, "Queen Victoria the Second, bless her time shots, is scheduled to open the new session of Parliament. As an Englishman, one's heart warms to the thought of traditional pageantry. But, at times it can be rather dull. The Lost Legion has decided to introduce a more meaningful touch."

"How?"

"By translating it into a state funeral," said Leander. "A British sovereign has not, I believe, died by assassination in recent times. I am sure Victoria would be inordinately flattered to know that she had been selected to rectify the omission."

"You're stark and ultra staring."

"Certainly. But not uniquely so. Think of it, Dion. It's dramatic, it's bold, it's terrible and quite deliciously shocking. It's the kind of thing that will make half the doms of England blow their amplifier circuits."

"It's the kind of thing that will collect a sufficiency of grade ones to tranquilize the Lost Legion in its entirety."

"There are hazards, indeed," admitted Leander.

Dion gave him a wintry smile. "Let me guess who is supposed to chiefly enjoy them."

"It will be your last act," said Leander. "After this you may retire with honor."

"And a plateful of porridge where my brain used to be. No thank you. Let someone else gain glory—preferably yourself."

"What is this," asked Sylphide in helpless bewilderment, "some kind of funny exercise?"

"Yes, love, it's hilarious," explained Dion. "The gent here wants me to chop Victoria in exchange for nothing."

"In exchange for doing nothing," corrected Leander, looking significantly at Sylphide. "And also in exchange for guaranteeing a peaceful fecundity in your time."

"Normally," explained Dion, "he lives under a wet stone, but the run of dry weather has unsettled him."

"Of course," said Leander gently, raising the laser pistol, "if you are not interested in the welfare of the third and fourth generations—or even the second—we can settle the matter after a fashion here and now."

"Not so fast, scorpion. How do I know that this will be the last gambit?"

Leander sighed. "Is there no trust between us?"

"No."

"You sadden me. I have here a confession signed by myself that I personally am responsible for the dyeing of Parliament and the anticipated death of the Queen. It is your certificate of freedom. In the event of a slight misunderstanding, you or your good infra would, I presume, know what to do with it."

Dion gazed at the darkening sky and shivered. "It's colder than you think. Come inside and we'll discuss your little essay in treason over a glass or two of pain killer."

"Charmed, I'm sure," Leander tucked his laser pistol away. "Incidentally, if I do not return to London by midday tomorrow, you will be embarrassingly dead and therefore quite unable to contemplate the interesting future of any offspring, potential or actual. That would be sad, would it not?"

"Perhaps," conceded Dion. "Nevertheless, the sentiment has been registered."

Sylphide began to cry. "It's a nightmare," she sobbed. "It can't be like this. All we wanted to do was live and love and be alone. Why should anybody want to take it away?"

Dion kissed her gently. "That's the sixty-four milliard lion question, love." He glanced at Leander. "And the answer is quite simple. Because some bastard joker made it easier

129

for a rich dom to pass through the eye of a camel than for a poor sport to needle his way into the kingdom of heaven."

SEVENTEEN

It was a fine, still morning with a slight bouquet of frost in the wine-sharp air. Dion, in an iridescent sky suit and with a racing jet pack strapped to his back, lay flat on his face, the snout of his scoped laser rifle poking discreetly between the thick pillars of the low balustrade. The balustrade had been added to the flattened top of the Cenotaph in Whitehall during the early twenties, when vid was still more or less earthbound and state occasions had to be shot from solid coigns of vantage.

But now that ground controlled hover-cameras were used, Dion had the top of the Cenotaph all to himself—which was just as well, because even the sensation-hungry doms of Centrovid might have stopped short at aiding and abetting regicide.

He had been lying there since before daylight, and he was stiff with fear and stillness, having hardly moved during the last four hours. Despite the chameleonlike qualities of his sky suit, even the slightest movement might have been picked up by a drifting hover-camera or a patrolling Peace Officer, and then his ID digits would have been up. Even frustrated regicide would merit a grade one.

As he lay there, waiting for Leander's radio bleep from Admiralty Arch to signal that the procession was four minutes away, Dion had time to think about all the things he did not want to think about. Like how the next half-hour would probably see him permanently dead, anyway. If he

130

chopped Victoria, a lot of people would be justifiably annoyed, and if he did not chop her there were those who would also be somewhat annoyed. Thus it was merely a case of the devil or the deep blue yonder.

Leander's instructions had been explicit and nothing if not unequivocal. "Permanent, not temporary death is required, dearest boy," he had said. "If Victoria survives, she'll be a lousy heroine. So you either burn her head off or cut her in two. Monarchy, in this lovely dom's world, has to be seen to be a hazardous occupation."

The escape plan was simple enough to succeed—if it could be gotten off the ground. As soon as Leander had given his signal from Admiralty Arch, he would jet to the roof of the New Peace House, parallel to the Cenotaph, and wait for Dion to start burning. Then, as Dion lifted from the Cenotaph with his racing jets at full scream, Leander would create a small diversion and try to cut down any pursuing Peace Officers. Finally, the two of them would rendezvous at ten thousand feet—hopefully two thousand feet more than Peace Officers would dare to rise—and jet north together. Over Cambridgeshire, assuming they had thrown off all pursuit, they would separate. They would touch down at a deserted barn, where Leander had already stashed conventional rented sky gear, dump their rifles and racing kit, and say a briefly moving farewell to each other forever. Then Dion would lift north to Wits' End and Leander would lift south to London—two innocent squires going about their lawful occasions.

It was a reasonable plan—but one which Dion already knew was not going to work. It was not going to work because to make something like that work you had to want it to work. And, as always, he did not quite know what he wanted.

So he lay there sweating, with the cold air bathing his face, listening to the muted murmur of traffic and the nearer sounds of the infras and sports who had been paid a lion or two to cheer the Queen's progress already lining the route.

131

But for Stopes' sake! Why burn her? Would the frying of Victoria topple the entire monstrous regiment of women? It would not. It would merely stir the bitches up a bit. So why the ferkinell?

Answer: Because D. Quern had entered upon a somewhat improbable pact with the devil's disciple. Or because D. Quern had developed *joie de mourir*. Or because D. Quern was plain bored.

The radio bleep from Leander came through the microceiver lodged in his ear, and D. Quern jumped like a startled rabbit. The movement would surely be noticed. But it wasn't. He was rather disappointed.

"*Bon chance*, sport," whispered Leander's crackly voice. "The sausage is yours for the cooking. Give it Fahrenheit two thousand with love. . . . See you on top of the clouds, wonder boy. Out."

"Or in Hades," growled Dion to himself, "making like a microminiaturized snowball."

He raised himself cautiously up on one knee, his head still lower than the top of the balustrade, and peeped between the pillars. The carriage, preceded by half a squadron of Household Cavalry, their shaped metal breastplates bounding and glinting like a multiplicity of twin voracious eyes in the vague sunlight, turned into Whitehall.

Dion was trembling. The laser rifle felt simultaneously like a white-hot poker and a rod that weighed ten metric tons.

Sir Dion Quern, he thought, having recently received a knighthood, the royal bounty, and the intimate attention of the Queen's own person, did thereafter brood upon these injuries and resolve to bring to a permanent death the body of his most gracious liege sovereign. Therefore let his name be expunged from the records forever. And, despite the demise of Her Majesty, it shall be as if the sick-psych had never been misconceived.

He raised the laser rifle unsteadily and looked through the scope. Victoria, at two hundred meters and 10X, was smiling. Graciously. In the great tradition of British monarchs. They had smiled graciously for too many bleeding centuries. Now was the time to do some little something about it.

Dion notched back to maximum power, settled his cheek against the stock of the rifle, and peered through the scope once more. The breast-eyes on the cuirasses of the Household Cavalry danced hypnotically. Goddammit, there were rainbows all over the place. Goddammit, it must be raining. Goddammit, it wasn't raining. Goddammit, he was crying!

He tried to press the fire stud, but his finger was frozen like a petrified question mark.

One hundred and fifty yards. Victoria's smile was the smile of the sphinx. Anyone not a certifiable idiot could see she was as bored as hell. It would be an act of mercy to relieve her boredom.

The paid sports and infras lining the route began to cheer themselves hoarse and stupid, secure in the comfortable prospect of an imminence of alcohol. A number of feeble-minded doms were tossing handfuls of plastic rose petals. The vid cameras hovered like a swarm of giant flies.

He tried to press the fire stud again, and failed.

It was ridiculous.

It was ridiculous that a grown man could not execute a grown woman who was the symbol of feminine power in this dom-happy world into which he had been thrust.

One hundred yards. He brushed the tears away and tried hating her.

It didn't work. With a tremendous mental effort, he superimposed Juno's face on that of Victoria's. That didn't work either. His finger was frozen like a question mark that would never uncurl.

Then suddenly he thought of his mother, who had died of an embolism and seventeen pregnancies. Who had killed herself to buy him an education and a little time. And he was filled with a righteous anger.

Queen Victoria the Second of England was a symbol of the society that had made such a sacrifice necessary. It was time, therefore, for Victoria to collect, on behalf of all the doms she represented, the interest on the seventeenth pan of afterbirth.

Dion Quern stood up on the top of the Cenotaph. The Cenotaph itself represented ten million dead men. They had not died for anything glorious, whatever the historians tried to invent. Nor did they die so that a debased breed of women should inherit the earth.

Somehow, he sensed that they were with him. And there was a majority verdict.

He brushed away the tears and looked through the scope. His brain was cold and the question mark on the end of his hand was flexible. Victoria was still smiling.

The question mark tightened, and the smile vaporized. The horses reared. A few breastplates clanged deliciously on the roadway. The cheering seemed to swell into an ovation. And ten light-years away, on the roof of a building opposite, Leander Smith was chopping vainly with a laser pistol at the swarm of Peace Officers already jetting toward the top of the Cenotaph.

Dion did not move. He did not even want to move. He dropped the laser rifle and just stood there waiting.

He did not have to wait long.

Within thirty seconds he had been beaten into an unconscious pulp.

Within the same thirty seconds, Leander Smith realized that Dion no longer had any intention of jetting up to a rendezvous at ten thousand feet. But by that time he had left his own escape a little too late. Even as he began to rise, an enterprising dom burned off his jet pack with a lucky sweep from four hundred yards. He fell back on to the roof and broke his ankle.

He sat there waiting for them, laughing at the great shaggy assassination joke. Laughing quite hysterically at the inevitable prospect of grade one.

EIGHTEEN

The room was small, white, and bare. There were no windows. Artificial light with a greenish tint emanated from some source behind a circular metal grille in the ceiling. The metal door was magnetically locked. Two hard chairs were fixed magnetically to the floor. Dion Quern, hastily patched up from his impromptu beating, sat on one of them, and Leander Smith, nursing the tension-spray bandage on his foot, sat on the other.

Dion was trying to recollect the morning's events through a fog of pain and confusion. "I suppose I killed her?" he inquired at length.

Leander grimaced, and shifted his foot. "That you did, my son. Quite permanently. It is some small consolation in our present sorrow. Why the Stopes didn't you jet?"

"I don't know," said Dion. Then he added as an afterthought, "Maybe because I knew I'd killed her." He became angry. "Why didn't your lousy Lost Legion supply some more dedicated assassin? And in any case, it was not the task for a tottery twosome such as we."

"Interesting," mused Leander. "You have a tendency to alliterate in times of stress."

"Stuff the alliteration. Now that we're finished, your little Lost Legion will have to unearth other zombies its miscarriages to perform. That, at least, affords fractional consolation."

"There is no Lost Legion," said Leander somberly, "It surrendered this morning."

Dion's mouth opened, but it was some time before the

135

words came out. "What of the revolutionary army? What of the High Command?"

Leander smiled. "Little one, I was the High Command. You were the entire army corps—including cavalry and secret weapon."

There was a further silence while Dion swallowed and inwardly digested.

"So *you* planted the bomb in my tin heart?"

"There is no bomb in your tin heart."

"What about the homing device?"

"There is no homing device."

"Then how the Stopes did you know where I would be? That time in St. James's Park and then at Wits' End."

"Intelligence plus patience plus gullibility equals miracles," explained Leander. "I knew you were at Buck House, so I simply waited and followed you when you left. It was time-consuming, but the stakes were high. As for your little gray house in the north, all I had to do was lock onto Dom Juno, so to speak—who, I may add, jets like one dispossessed. . . . *Quod erat faciendum,* as one might say. Or perhaps *inveniendum* would be more appropriate."

"At the Clinic you demonstrated that you could kill me."

"Sweet child, I borrowed a servocardiac interrupter from a careless domdoc. They're standard equipment for testing electromechanical hearts. The absolute range is, I believe, ten yards. And the absolute limit for induced death is forty seconds. After that time, the emergency pump in your tin heart takes over."

"So it was all a con," said Dion weakly.

"May I suggest that you conned yourself—with minimal assistance."

"Why—for crysake?"

"Who knows?" said Leander, beginning to enjoy himself. "Who knows? Maybe you just wanted to be a zero hero."

"Not me, graverobber, you," explained Dion coldly. "Why you? Why this Lost Legion ploy? Why this compulsion to recruit one Dion Quern as a protagonist in your private fantasy? Why paint doms purple, burn the Queen, and set

136

it all up for someone to stir the porridge in what passes for your brain?"

Leander laughed. "Questions! Questions! Let us see if there are any satisfactory answers. One: the Lost Legion ploy. As an ex-poet, you will surely accept my plea of romanticism. Two: the recruitment of Dion Quern. Is it not enough, dear playmate, that I liked your face, to say nothing of your spirit? Three: why paint doms purple, etcetera. Gestures, my son. Less than magnificent, perhaps, but still gestures. I regret nothing. And on behalf of you, I regret nothing. We are as we are, and we presumed to be men. The meal was excellent, and now there is the reckoning. It would be churlish to complain."

Dion did not know whether to laugh or cry. But he met Leander's gaze, and the impulse to laughter won.

The sound of it reverberated harshly in the small bare room. Listening to it almost objectively even as he was convulsed in the act of producing it, Dion relished what would probably be his last boisterous guffaw at the mazy-dazy cosmos. But it was more than a guffaw and less than laughter. It was a heavily disguised cry from the heart. Eventually he calmed down sufficiently to realize that Leander was speaking again.

"I was quite a patient nihilist," said Leander. "I moiled, toiled, and boiled eleven years at the Trafalgar Square Clinic, waiting for the right kind of Lancelot to dive head first and with a wild shout into this plethora of dragons. Then you came along for time shots with a faceful of misery and a psychofile that showed three grade threes. I said to myself: This is the boyo. Here is a bright bouncy lad with an excess of adrenalin and enough imagination to swallow the totally absurd. How right I was. How wrongly right I was. You had just the combination of high intelligence and excessive stupidity to assume the posture of the Light Brigade when I said charge."

"There were others?" inquired Dion.

"There were others. In the course of years, there were others. Some I expended on small pranks like livening up baby farms. Some I sent on fanciful missions to foreign parts—you know the sort of thing: Sports of the world, unite; you have nothing to lose but your one-night stands. . . . But you—you had genuine potential. You made the joke worthwhile. You had a touch of artistry that almost made it credible—even to me."

"It could have been credible," said Dion slowly. "It could still be credible. Somewhere there might be a magnacolor stereophonic three-dee Lost Legion waiting for the final shout."

"Dion, dear innocent, you were born a fool," retorted Leander. "Kindly do not try to outdo nature. You have seen surely that there are no gentlemen left in England, and all the rest are now abed. For there are more beds than bodies in this demi-sec paradise. You cannot make a deaf-aid out of a silk kimono. Guts are obsolete. Pranksters play—viz the late revels at Stonehenge—but no one fights. Fighting needs guts, and guts are as aforementioned. We can prick the doms' bottoms, but we can't fight anymore. Hell, Master Ridley, we can't even light a decent candle, you and I. The cunning bitches have cheated us by throwing out capital punishment and keeping the death sentence. We shall wear our grade ones like clowns' hats and collect a backside kick from every oat-fed eunuch. But," he laughed, "the meal was excellent and the nonvintage wine had a briefly amusing presumption. Amen."

There was a silence.

"I suppose there will be a trial?" said Dion, at length.

"A reasonable supposition," returned Leander with some complacency. "Regicide is a dying art, but it still commands some small respect."

Dion laughed. "Guilty but inane."

Leander laughed also. "And that, sweet prince, is the verdict of us all."

"You realize, of course, that I only wanted to live in peace, that I had found something worth having, that I'd made a world where the twenty-first century didn't exist."

138

Leander was unmoved. "I saved you from becoming a vegetable."

"So that I could be transformed into another kind of vegetable."

"Possibly. But there was also something I had to know. It seemed important."

"What the Stopes could be that important?"

Briefly the mask fell from Leander's sardonic face. "I had to know if we were men. . . . And I did not want to be alone."

Then they heard the sound of approaching footsteps in the corridor outside.

NINETEEN

La reine est morte. Vive la reine.

Elizabeth the Third, having combined in her own superbly juvenile fifty-year-old body the joint persons of heir presumptive and heir apparent, succeeded the late martyr queen; and as her first public act attended the legal circus (one of the alltime highs of Intervid shows, with an estimated viewscore of nine hundred million) that was to dispose of those who had made her accession possible.

The trial lasted three hours and forty minutes, including intermission and natural breaks. It had been carefully placed in the peak viewing spot, Standard Federation Time, and therefore ruined several million dinner parties and similar mild social diversions. Both prisoners pleaded Guilty but Sane, and both pleas were rejected.

The nominal jury consisted of seven doms, two sports, one squire, and two infras, all good citizens and true, each being granted permanent relief from jury service thereafter and one half of one per cent interest in the vid rights, still-pix, dramatization rights, and transcript sales for a period of five years. It had been estimated that gross earnings (an American dom had already bid a clear half em for the musical version) would touch one million lions.

Leander performed with his customary verve, and Dion made two short but moving orations on the rights of man. The actual verdict was unanimous: Guilty but Insane. And the viewdict, recorded by the Intervid computer showed: Guilty but Insane, three hundred and forty-two million, two hundred and ten thousand, three hundred and seventeen. Guilty but Sane, nine hundred and two thousand and forty-three; Innocent, one hundred and four.

Donning her black silk shift, the judge directed that the prisoners be removed to a place of contemplation for three clear Sundays before being taken thence to suffer the blessed relief and total absolution of grade one analysis, together with the permanent suspension of time shots. Leander, protesting violently at being denied capital punishment, had to be removed from the court forcibly by four smilingly efficient doms who did not hit him until they were out of vid range. Dion blew a kiss to the Queen, thumbed his nose at the judge—whose silk-covered breast was heaving rhythmically for the benefit of vid close-ups—and left the court under his own steam.

He did not see Leander again. They were taken to separate cells. Leander, declaring himself to be a devout Muslim, requested a prayer mat. He spent the next two days secretly unraveling it and fashioning a tolerably strong noose. On the third day, he hanged himself, thus registering in the strongest possible terms his complete disapproval of the abolition of capital punishment. He had cunningly timed his demise so that discovery would be too late to give the resuscitation doms a chance of retaliating with resurrection. However, his final gesture was neutralized by a vid release which claimed that he had suffered massive cerebral hemorrhage occasioned by agonies of remorse and repentance.

Neither Sylphide nor Juno had attended or watched the trial—for different reasons. The shock of the assassination and the capture of Dion was sufficient to cause Sylphide, still living at Wits' End, to miscarry. Since she was only a few weeks pregnant, this was, in purely physical and medical terms, a very small happening. But for Sylphide, whom Dion had taught to love and to be proud that she would one day bear a child that she could call her own, it was the end of the world. On top of Dion's capture and imminent grade one, it became too much for her already overloaded neural circuits. She grabbed the nearest sharp instrument that came to hand (a pair of antique scissors that Dion had acquired to go with the antique world he was creating in his antique house) and struck out. Or, rather, struck in.

There had been a memorable phrase in an old book from which Dion used to read to her: *If thine eye offend thee, pluck it out and cast it from thee.*

Her womb had offended. It had betrayed her, Dion, and the future. So in a frenzy of grief, she took the scissors and stabbed with hate and anger at the smooth white belly that had rejected her son. She stabbed until pain and anguish and the fog in her mind turned the world coolly and sweetly dark.

She would probably have bled to death—though, surprisingly, none of the wounds was fatal—if Juno had not arrived that same evening, having jetted up to Wits' End to comfort her after the verdict had been reached. Juno found her lying in the bathroom, with the scissors still clutched tightly in her thin white hand. Fifteen minutes later Sylphide was in the South Manchester Clinic with the domdocs arguing as to how much resection of the intestines there would be and whether a synthetic stomach was required. In the end they managed to patch her up. Sylphide, without any knowledge of anatomy, had aimed well. A hysterectomy had to be performed. *If thine eye offend thee, pluck it out. . . .*

And now she lay in bed at the Clinic, recovering in body if not in mind.

And Leander lay in a plastic coffin, oblivious of the final joke. For his passage into the cleansing fire of the Greater London Crematorium (Alien Religions Division) was attended by thirty-one Muslims, two muezzins, and a self-styled latter-day prophet.

And Juno, having been granted a pretreatment visit, jetted to Her Majesty's Major Analysis Center for Disoriented and Asocial Persons.

And Dion, having been left incommunicado, knew nothing about anything.

Their meeting took place after the third clear Sunday, and two days before grade one analysis was due to begin. It was a short visit, Juno being allowed ten minutes only. He didn't even want to see her; but since she was armed with Authority, his wishes were of no account.

He did not look up when she came into his cell. But he looked up when she told him about Sylphide and then about Leander. And each saw that the other's face was wet with tears.

"Dion, there's something I want," said Juno softly.

He tried to laugh. "In exchange for the good news you bring?"

"In exchange for our memories of the good times," she retorted in an abnormally calm voice. "Because soon they will belong only to me."

Dion was silent for a moment or two. Then, "I've always heard you can't weep after a grade one. . . . It will be a vast improvement."

"You can't write poetry, either," said Juno. "Dion, there isn't much time . . . I want you to give me a semen donation."

"A what?"

"A semen donation. I—I want there to be more of your children."

This time he managed to laugh. Uproariously.

"By Emmeline, Marie, Victoria, and all the saints in the

142

great gray calendar, that is one overripe peach of a notion! Now will I believe in footsteps on the face of the water."

"Dion, please. There isn't much time."

"You are right, flat-belly, there isn't much time. There never was much time, not from the day I first met you to the day Leander sweet-talked me into a myth."

"Time was always the enemy of troubadours," she observed sadly. "That's why I want there to be more of your children."

"I want no children now," he said with bitterness. "I want nothing."

"This is not for you. It's for me."

"Can you give me one good reason why I should do anything for you?"

"I love you, that's all."

"It's not enough." Then he added after a moment, "But we can strike a bargain, you and I. You want something. I want nothing—except to know that someone will think for Sylphide, since she is incapable of thinking for herself."

"I'll think for Sylphide, then."

"She is to be quite free, you understand."

"Agreed."

"She will stay at Wits' End."

"Agreed."

"You will not see her unless she wants to see you."

"Agreed."

"Then you can have your semen donation—and God bless the wretched infras whose wombs will receive seed, the sowing of which brought no joy."

"I'll . . . I'll send someone to collect the sample."

He laughed. "Then you can stick it in a bottle labeled Hic Iacet Dion Quern, who ejaculated to the last."

Juno could bear it no longer. She turned to go. Then she paused. "Don't you want to know anything about Jubal —where he is, how he's progressing?"

Dion looked at her. "Who is Jubal?"

Juno knocked on the cell door, had it opened, and fled, hoping to get away from H.M. Major Analysis Center for

143

Disoriented and Asocial Persons before she broke down completely.

Her hopes were not fulfilled.

TWENTY

Night and day lost their meaning, and were swallowed and inwardly digested in the bleak black stomach of eternity. He lived for millennia—he *existed* for millennia—in a place that had no walls, no roof, no windows, no floor. The sound of his voice—and at first he screamed and shouted greatly—was absorbed by the padded sphere of darkness. He dreamed, he had nightmares, he talked to himself and to people who were not there.

Presently he was taken out of the disorientation sphere, and before he could recover his wits, he had an armful of needleholes, each hole representing a further measured dose of eternity.

Now he was in a world of multicolored lights, their patterns changing perpetually and hypnotically. Occasionally he was aware of other voices, other ghosts.

They came out of a mist. White, they came, talking softly so that he could not hear, talking about him. He strained his eyes but he could not see the faces. He strained his ears but he could not hear the words.

Slowly, patiently, the great machine of grade one analysis picked its way through the primitive psychic jungle that was called Dion Quern. The domdocs probed his memories, charted his weaknesses, all his experiences, all his joys and sorrows. The computer predicted his crises, arranged a program of progressive catharsis. Psychodramas were projected on the vacant screen of his mind, symbols were brought up and canceled. And fear by fear, grief by grief, joy by joy, triumph by triumph, the tensions and the hypertensions were eroded away.

He felt himself becoming empty. The plug had been taken out of the bottom of his soul, and the personal history of a man was draining out like cold bathwater gurgling through ancient pipes.

Night and day lost their meaning; and there was only the long emptying, leading to a long emptiness.

"Who are you?" a voice asked.

He was asleep or awake or both.

"Dion," he managed to say. "I am Dion." Then he stopped, exhausted.

"Dion what?"

Dion what? Dion what? *Dion what?*

He didn't know. He knew he should know. But he didn't know. He curled up to think about it. He fell asleep. Or awake.

"Who are you?" a voice asked.

"Yes," he said reasonably, "you are quite right."

"Who are you?"

"Dion . . . I think."

"Dion what?"

"Dion . . . Dion . . . Dion dying . . . Dying Dion." He began to laugh.

Time passed. History dissolved. Darkness was upon the face of the deep.

"Who are you?" asked the voice.

He was getting to love the voice. It was friendly and warm. Intimate. It might almost have been his own.

He screamed.

It was his own.

He screamed and curled up and thought about it. He fell asleep. Or awake. Or both.

A wind whistled and whispered through trees that were not there. A cat jumped over the void left by the absence of the moon. One hand clapped.

"Who are you?" asked a different voice.

"Why are you a different voice?" he inquired with casual interest.

"A different voice is a different man," answered the voice. "Who are you?"

"Not who, but what," he pointed out.

"What are you, then?"

"I am alone."

"How long have you been alone?"

"Since the beginning of the world."

"Whom do you love?"

"I love no one, because there is no one in the world."

"Whom do you hate?"

"I hate no one, because there is no one in the world."

"What do you want?"

"There is nothing to want."

"Why do you exist?"

He did not know. He wanted time to think about it. He curled up to think about it. He fell asleep thinking about it. He woke up thinking about it.

He found the answer. He was nothing.

"I exist because I am nothing," he said with some conviction. "My existence is imperfect because I am not yet the negation of nothing. If I could cease to think, I should be most perfectly nothing and the question of my existence would not arise."

"Then," said the voice, "you must strive not to think. Your name is Dion Quern. Think nothing of it. You are a man. Think nothing of it. You are alive. Think nothing of that also."

Dion sighed with contentment. He had arrived at the ultimate truth.

* * *

One cold, wet spring morning a man emerged from the closely guarded precincts of Her Majesty's Major Analysis Center for Disoriented and Asocial Persons. His name had

146

been tattooed on the inside of his left wrist, in case he should forget it.

He sniffed the damp cold air and shivered. This world outside the world was a strange and formidable place. He did not know what to do.

Someone was waiting for him. He did not know her.

"Hello, Dion," said Juno.

He looked at his wrist and saw that his name was indeed Dion. He smiled. It seemed a safe sort of thing to do.

"I'm going to take you home," said Juno. She knew what to expect. And she had promised herself that there would be no tears.

"Home?"

"A place where you used to live."

He thought about it for a while. Then he said cautiously, "I think I would like that. . . . What is home called?"

"Wits' End," said Juno. "It's a house called Wits' End."

He grinned. "Your face is wet," he said. "Has it been raining?"

He was immensely pleased. He had remembered about rain. It was water that fell from the sky.

EPITAPH

The old man had been a recluse for many years. Once there had been a woman living with him, but that had been a long time ago. How long, he did not remember. Sometimes he remembered her name. Sometimes he forgot that she had ever existed. Sometimes he heard her voice, and remembered that she had died.

He was alone with the hills and the sky, alone in an old

147

house that would have looked to anyone else like a mauso-
leum.

He thought he was a farmer. He had a few hens and a
few sheep and a rusty plough and an antique tractor that
wouldn't work. One of these days he was going to fix the
tractor and plough up half of his five-acre field. Then he
could grow corn for the hens. One of these days.

He had no money, but every week groceries and beer
were delivered to his house. And corn for the hens. The
supplies were delivered in the night, and he always found
them on the doorstep in the morning. He did not know
where they came from or who sent them. They had been
delivered so regularly over the years that he ceased to think
about them. They were as natural as sunset and winter,
as natural as hunger and sleep.

Sometimes he saw people, but mostly he saw nobody. He
didn't mind. In the daytime there was much to be done.
In the evenings there were books to read and music to
listen to. It was easy enough to read the same book over
and over again, because by the time he had reached the end
he had usually forgotten the beginning.

Occasionally the words disturbed him. Because occasionally they sounded strangely like music. He would form
them laboriously, speak them out aloud, wondering at something that he did not understand. Something that he would
once have recognized as rhythm and cadence.

> *For though they be punished in the sight of men,*
> *yet is their hope full of immortality.*
> *And having been a little chastised,*
> *they shall be greatly rewarded:*
> *for God proved them,*
> *and found them worthy for himself.*

He did not fully understand the meaning of such words;
but he knew that in them there was something of beauty.

One day a woman jetted into the valley from the south.
He did not know her. He knew only that she seemed young
and full of energy, and her hair glinted gold in the sunlight.

148

She held out her hand. He didn't know whether to take it or kiss it or do both. So he did nothing.

"It's been a long time, Dion," she said.

He looked at the name on his wrist and knew that she knew him.

"Yes," he said cautiously. "It has been a long time."

"Once you gave me something."

"I did?"

"You did. And in a little while, I shall be giving you something back . . . You don't remember me at all, do you?"

"No. I don't remember. . . . I'm sorry. . . . Is there something I should remember?"

"It doesn't matter. I'm going to tell you something, Dion. Perhaps you won't understand much, but it doesn't matter. It is something I want to tell you. . . . A long time ago, when you were young, you were full of fire and wonderful words. You had to live in a world dominated by women, and you hated it. You hated the women, but also you loved them. In the end you did something terrible—for which the women took away all your fire and all your wonderful words. Do you understand?"

"Good dom," he said anxiously, remembering his manners, "I have never been a man of fire. And the only words I know that are beautiful are the words I have read in books. I hope I did nothing wrong?"

"Dion," said Juno, "there was something they could not destroy. Something terrible, something glorious. They could not destroy the secret of your seed."

"My seed?"

"Your seed. The seed that is passed from generation to generation. You are a freak, Dion, a genetic miracle. There was more to your dreams than we thought . . . Don't even try to understand what I mean. I am not even sure that I understand too clearly, myself. But you have double-Y chromosomes, and the pattern is somehow dominant. It is enough for you to know that you can only breed sons."

"Sons?" He gazed at her uncomprehendingly.

149

"Yes, sons. You gave me your seed, and the seed has produced nothing but sons."

"Sons?" he said again. Echoes were reverberating down the long corridors of memory. There was a curious aching in his chest—a sensation that he had not experienced for far longer than he could remember.

"You have eight sons, Dion, tall and strong." Juno spread out her hands apologetically. "There might have been more, but they were all I could afford. Each son has a different mother but each has the same father. They have been told about their father and"—she smiled—"since there was much that was wonderful in a meistersinger that I once knew, they are not ashamed."

"Eight sons," he repeated mechanically. There seemed to be a drumroll inside his ancient ribs, and the drumroll swelled into thunder.

"Eight sons," echoed Juno. "And three of them have the dominant double-Y chromosomes. They too can breed only sons. . . . So it seems that you have won the war, Dion, in a way that no one ever dreamed you could have won. Your sons will breed more sons. And in the end, if we do not make any more mistakes, we can create a balanced world of men and women."

"Eight sons," said Dion. He was an old man, and he understood nothing of double-Y chromosomes; but whatever else it could do, grade one analysis could not destroy the ancient music of the blood.

"I gave them names you might once have liked," went on Juno. "I called them Blake, Byron, and Shelley; Marlowe, Tennyson, Eliot and Thomas. . . ." She gave a faint smile. "The first of all was Jubal."

"Where are they?" demanded Dion. "Where are my sons?"

"Waiting only for me to call them. You see, I—I wanted to talk to you first. . . . I wanted to know if—" Her voice faltered.

Briefly the mists cleared a little in Dion's mind. Briefly he sensed that this stranger was no stranger, not a ghost even, but someone with whom he had shared a brighter world—before a name was tattooed on his wrist.

"Thank you," he said simply. "Forgive me. There is something I know and can't remember. . . . Forgive me. Will you call my sons?"

Juno spoke into the tiny transceiver clipped to her sky suit.

Presently eight dark shapes swooped in formation from the south. They circled low over Wits' End, then touched down together in front of Juno and Dion.

The old man gazed at their proud, young faces. He saw the brightness in their eyes and sensed the energy in their limbs. Truly, they were men.

And then he thought briefly and vaguely of the dark fog of forgetfulness and loneliness in which he had lived for so many years. And the words that had obscurely comforted him for so long came tumbling into his mind:

> *For though they be punished in the sight of men,*
> *yet is their hope full of immortality.*
> *And having been a little chastised,*
> *they shall be greatly rewarded. . . .*

Dion Quern, having endured much, and remembering little, realized dimly at last that the journey had been worthwhile.

He held out his hands. "Welcome," he said. "Welcome, all my sons."

It was late autumn, and there was a touch of frost in the air.

But there was also the strange, autumnal scent of fulfillment.